The Ivory Snuff Box

By Frederic Arnold Kummer

Writing As

Arnold Fredericks

Originally published in 1912

The Ivory Snuff Box

© 2014 Resurrected Press
www.ResurrectedPress.com

Published by Resurrected Press

This classic book was handcrafted by Resurrected Press. Resurrected Press is dedicated to bringing high quality classic books back to the readers who enjoy them. These are not scanned versions of the originals, but, rather, quality checked and edited books meant to be enjoyed!

Please visit ResurrectedPress.com to view our entire catalogue!

ISBN 13: 978-1-937022-48-8

Printed in the United States of America

FOREWORD

There are a number of interesting facets to Frederic Arnold Kummer's *The Ivory Snuff Box*. The mystery reflects the heightened international tensions of the period just before the First World War. Though never explicitly mentioned, Germany is seen as the menace, with a network of agents already in place in capitols across the continent. Against this threat is an alliance between France and Britain, never an easy partnership. The situation in Morocco, where a rebellion has been brewing, is the immediate focus, but the stresses that would result in the outbreak of war two years later are the real background for the story.

Of perhaps more interest to the reader of mysteries, *The Ivory Snuff Box* involves what may very well be the first husband-wife detective duo in the genre. Richard Duvall, an American detective working for the French police, and his wife Grace were first introduced to readers and to each other in *One Million Francs*. In that story, Duvall rescues Grace from the clutches of her step-uncle who sought to deprive her of her inheritance by marrying her off to his ner-do-well nephew, by disguising himself as an apache trying to extort money from the step-uncle. In his role as a French detective he resolves the situation by arresting himself for his own murder, and of course marrying Grace. The Duvalls would feature in a number of other mysteries by Kummer, which appeared originally under his pseudonym Arnold Fredericks, in which Grace plays an active part in her husbands adventures.

In what may be another first, the plot device of checking into an asylum run by the chief suspect is also used in *The Ivory Snuff Box*. This, of course, lends itself to many dramatic possibilities, which Kummer takes advantage of. The doctor running the asylum has been experimenting with ultra-violet rays as a tool for treating mental disorders but discovers that they can also be used as a torture device, leading to some very cinematic scenes. It is not surprising, then, that Kummer would soon turn his hand to screenwriting for the fledgling motion picture industry.

Frederic Arnold Kummer is not well known today, but in the early twentieth century he was a popular and successful author, playwright, and screen writer. In *The Ivory Snuff Box* he presents us with a lively tale of intrigue and danger. It is with pleasure that Resurrected Press offers you this new edition of *The Ivory Snuff Box*.

About the Author

Frederic Arnold Kummer (August 5, 1873-November 22, 1943) was an American author, playwright and screen writer. Born in Maryland, he studied engineering at Rensselaer Polytechnic Institute, and worked as an engineer before turning to writing in 1907. He wrote in a variety of genres including romances and non-fiction. Under the pseudonym Arnold Fredericks he wrote a series of mysteries featuring the detective Richard Duvall. In the 1930's he turned to writing science fiction. In addition to his short stories and novels he was also a screen writer during the early days of motion pictures. On a curious note, shortly after his death during World War II he had a Liberty ship was named after him.

Greg Fowlkes
Editor-In-Chief
Resurrected Press
www.ResurrectedPress.com

TABLE OF CONTENTS

CHAPTER I

The last thing that sounded in Richard Duvall's ears as he left the office of Monsieur Lefevre, Prefect of Police of Paris, were the latter's words, spoken in a voice of mingled confidence and alarm, "The fortunes of a nation may depend upon your faithfulness. Go, and God be with you." He entered the automobile which was drawn up alongside the curb, and accompanied by Vernet, one of the Prefect's assistants, was soon threading the torrent of traffic which pours through the *Rue de Rivoli*.

The thoughts which lay uppermost in the detective's mind were of Grace, his wife; Grace Ellicott, who had become Grace Duvall but little more than an hour before. By this time he had expected to be on his way to Cherbourg, *en route* to New York, with Grace by his side. They had looked forward so happily to their honeymoon, on shipboard, and now—he found himself headed for London on this mysterious expedition, and Grace waiting for him in vain at the *pension*. The thought was maddening. He swore softly to himself as he looked out at the crowded street.

Monsieur Lefevre had no right to ask so great a sacrifice of him, he grumbled. What if he had distinguished himself, made himself the Prefect's most valued assistant, during the past six or eight months? The matters which had brought him from New York to Paris had all been definitely concluded—Grace and he were married—his plans had all been made, to return to America, and home. Now at the last moment, it was frightfully exasperating to have Monsieur Lefevre insist that matters of so grave a nature had occurred, that the honor of his very country was at stake, and to call upon him, Duvall, as the one man who could set matters right.

Of course, it was very flattering, but he wanted, not flattery, but Grace, and all the happiness which lay before them. What, after all, was this matter, this affair so vague and mysterious, into which he had so unexpectedly been thrown? He drew out the instructions which the Prefect had hurriedly thrust into his hands, and looked at them with eager curiosity.

They covered but one side of a small sheet of paper. "Visit immediately number 87, *Rue de Richelieu*," they said. "It is a small curio shop. Monsieur Dufrenne, the proprietor, expects you, and will join you at once. Proceed without delay to London and report to Monsieur de Grissac, the French Ambassador. He has lost an ivory snuff box, which you must recover as quickly as possible. You will find money enclosed herewith. Monsieur Dufrenne you can trust in all things. God be with you.— Lefevre."

It was the first time that Duvall had read the instructions. He had not had an opportunity to do so before. As he concluded his examination of them, his face hardened, his brow contracted in a frown, and he crushed the piece of paper in his hand. Was this some absurd joke that Monsieur Lefevre was playing upon him? The idea of separating him from Grace upon their wedding day, to send him on an expedition, the object of which was to recover a lost snuff box! It seemed preposterous. In his anger he muttered an exclamation which attracted the attention of Vernet. He was, in fact, on the point of stopping the automobile, and going at once to the *pension* where Grace was waiting for him, her trunks packed for their wedding journey. The impassive face of the Frenchman beside him relaxed a trifle, as he saw Duvall's agitation. "What is it, Monsieur Duvall?" he inquired.

"Do you know anything about this matter that makes it necessary for me to go to London?" demanded Duvall.

"Nothing, monsieur, except that your train leaves—" he consulted his watch—"in twenty minutes."

Duvall drew out a cigar and lit it, with a gesture of annoyance. "The matter does not appear very important," he grumbled.

Vernet permitted a slight smile to cross his usually immobile face. "I have been in the service of the Prefect for ten years," he remarked, "and I have learned that he wastes very little time upon unimportant things." He leaned out and spoke to the chauffeur, and in a moment the car halted before a dingy little shop, on the lower floor of an old and dilapidated-looking house. "Here is the place of Monsieur Dufrenne," he remarked significantly.

Duvall threw open the door of the cab, and entered the dusty and cobwebbed doorway. He found himself in a small dimly lighted room, so crowded with curios of all sorts that he at first did not perceive the little white-haired old man who bent over a jeweler's work bench in one corner. The walls were lined with shelves, upon which stood bits of ivory and porcelain, miniatures of all sorts, old pieces of silverware, bronze and copper, old coins, and rusty antique weapons. About the walls stood innumerable pictures, old and cracked, in dilapidated-looking frames, while from the ceiling were suspended bits of rusty armor, swords, brass censers, Chinese lamps, and innumerable other objects, the use of which he could scarcely guess.

All these things he saw, in a queer jumble of impressions, as his eyes swept the place. In a moment the little old man in the corner turned, peering at him over his steel-rimmed spectacles. "You wish to see me, monsieur?" he inquired in a thin, cracked voice.

"Yes. I am Richard Duvall. I come from Monsieur the Prefect of Police."

The man at the workbench, on hearing these words, rose to his insignificant height, dropping as he did so the watch over which he had been working. He swept his tools into a drawer with a single gesture, turned to the wall behind him, drew on a thin gray overcoat and a dark slouch hat, and stepped from behind the counter. "I am ready, monsieur," he remarked, without a trace of agitation or excitement. "Let us go."

Duvall turned to the door without further words, and threw it open. The old man motioned to him to pass out, and after the detective had done so, closed and locked the door carefully and followed him into the cab. Duvall observed that he was frail, and uncertain in his steps, and so bent from constant labor over his bench, that he gave one almost the impression of being hunchbacked. He took his seat beside the detective without a word, and in a moment the whole party was being driven rapidly toward the *Gare du Nord*.

Duvall could not repress a feeling of admiration for the way in which Dufrenne had received him. He had asked no questions, delayed him by no preparations, but had merely thrown down his tools, put on his hat, and started out. The importance or lack of importance of the matters which called him he did not inquire into—it was evidently quite enough, that Monsieur Lefevre desired his services. It made the detective feel somewhat ashamed of his recent ill nature, yet he could not but remember that this was his wedding day, and that in leaving his wife without even so much as a farewell word, he had given her good reason for doubting his love for her. Of course, he knew, the Prefect had assured him that he would explain everything to Grace, but such explanations were not likely to appeal very strongly to a girl who had been married but little more than an hour. It was, therefore, in a very dissatisfied frame of mind that he entered the compartment of the train for Boulogne.

The compartment was a smoking one, and he and Dufrenne had it all to themselves. The little old Frenchman drew out a much-stained meerschaum pipe and began placidly to smoke it. His manner toward the detective was respectful, friendly indeed, yet he made no attempts at conversation, and seemed quite satisfied to sit and gaze out of the car window at the fields and villages as they swept by. Presently Duvall spoke.

"Monsieur Dufrenne," he began, slowly, "you are no doubt familiar with the matter which takes us to London?"

Dufrenne withdrew his gaze from the window and faced about in his seat with a nervous little gesture of assent. "I understand that Monsieur de Grissac has been robbed of his snuff box," he replied.

"Is that all you know?" Duvall inquired pointedly. "Surely the recovery of an article of so little consequence cannot be the real purpose of our visit."

The little old man shrugged his shoulders, with an almost imperceptible gesture of dissent. "I know nothing of the matter, monsieur," he remarked, significantly, "except that my country has called me, and that I am here." He spoke the words proudly, as though he considered the fact that he had been called upon an honor.

"But surely, you must have some idea, monsieur, of your purpose in being here?"

"Yes. That is indeed quite simple. On one occasion I was called upon to repair the snuff box of Monsieur de Grissac, the Ambassador. In that way I am familiar with its appearance. Now that it is lost, I am requested to accompany you, monsieur, in your attempt to recover it, in order that I may assist you in identifying it."

"And beyond that, you know nothing?"

"Nothing, monsieur."

Duvall began to chew the end of his cigar in vexation. Of all the absurd expeditions, this seemed the most absurd. Presently he turned to Dufrenne and again spoke. "In your repairs upon this snuff box, to which so great a value is apparently attached, did you observe anything about it of a peculiar nature—anything to make its loss a matter of such grave importance?"

"Nothing, monsieur. It is a small, round ivory box, with a carved top, quite plain and of little value—"

"But the contents? What, perhaps, did Monsieur de Grissac carry within it?"

"Snuff, monsieur. It was quite half-full when it came to me, last April. Monsieur de Grissac was in Paris at the time. The spring which actuates the top had become broken—the box is very old, monsieur—and I was required to repair it. That is all I know."

"And you close your shop, and leave Paris without a word, just for a thing like that?"

Dufrenne straightened his bent shoulders, and his eyes sparkled. "When France calls me, monsieur, I have nothing to do but obey."

His reply seemed almost in the nature of a reproof. Duvall made no further comment and relapsed into a brown study. After all, he knew, even in his irritation, that Monsieur Lefevre had not sent him upon this adventure without some real and very good reason. Yet try as he would, he was unable to imagine what this reason could be. Of course, there must have been something inside the box, his final conclusion was, else why should any one have stolen it? No doubt the Ambassador, Monsieur de Grissac, would acquaint him with the truth of the affair. Possibly the box may have contained papers of great value—though why one should choose such a place for the concealment of valuable papers he could not imagine. The whole affair seemed shrouded in mystery, and no amount of speculation on his part, apparently, would throw any light upon it. He lay back in his seat, dozing, and thinking of Grace and their interrupted honeymoon.

At Boulogne they transferred to the boat for Folkstone, and after a quiet passage, found themselves on board the train for London. They reached Charing Cross early in the evening, and taking a cab, drove at once to Monsieur de Grissac's residence in Piccadilly, opposite Green Park.

CHAPTER II

While Richard Duvall was thus flying toward
Boulogne, racking his brains in a futile attempt to
discover the reasons for his sudden and unexpected
dispatch to London, Grace, his wife, equally mystified,
was proceeding in the direction of Brussels.

The reasons for her going to Brussels were no more
clear to her than were Richard's, to him. At the
conclusion of the wedding breakfast which had followed
her simple marriage to Duvall, she had gone to the
pension at which she had been living, to await her
husband's return. She had not then understood the
mysterious message which had summoned him to the
Prefect's office, nor, for that matter, had he, but he had
assured her that he would return in a short while, and
that had been enough for her.

Her patient waiting had been finally terminated by
the arrival of the Prefect himself, who had explained with
polite brevity that a matter of the gravest importance had
made it necessary for him to send Richard at once to
London.

The girl's grief and alarm had been great—Monsieur
Lefevre had at last, however, succeeded in convincing her
that Richard could not under the circumstances have
done anything but go. His position as an assistant to
Lefevre, and more particularly the friendship which
existed between them, made it imperative for him to
come to the Prefect's assistance in this crisis.

What the crisis was, Grace did not learn. She had
insisted upon following Richard, upon being near him,
upon assisting him, should opportunity offer, and
Monsieur Lefevre, seized with a sudden inspiration, had
dispatched her to Brussels, with the assurance that she

would not only see her husband very soon, but might be able to render both him, and France, a very signal service.

Grace had accepted the mission; her desire to be near Richard was a compelling motive, and as a result she found herself flying toward the Belgian frontier, on an early afternoon express, with no idea whatever of what lay before her, and only a few words, written by Monsieur Lefevre upon a page torn from his notebook, to govern her future actions.

She luckily was able to find a compartment in one of the first-class carriages where she could be alone, and sank back upon the cushioned seat, determined to face whatever dangers the future might hold, for the sake of her husband.

Her mind traveled, in retrospect, over the events of the past few months—the conspiracy against her, by her step-uncle, Count d'Este, by which he had so nearly deprived her of the fortune left to her by her aunt, and the striking way in which his plans had been upset by Richard Duvall. She had loved him at their very first meeting, and now that they had become husband and wife, she loved him more than ever. It is small wonder that the thought of the way in which he had been suddenly torn from her, on the eve of their wedding journey, brought tears to her eyes.

Presently she regained her composure and looked at the sheet of paper which the Prefect had handed to her. It contained but a few words: "Proceed to the Hotel Metropole, Brussels. Take a room in the name of Grace Ellicott, and wait further instructions." That was all—no hint of how or when she and Richard were to meet, or what had been the cause of their separation. Once more the cruelty of the situation brought tears to her eyes. While feeling in her handbag for her handkerchief, she drew out the small silver ring which the Prefect had handed to her at the last moment. "Trust any one," he had said, "who comes to you with such a token as this."

She examined the ring carefully, but the singular device worked in gold upon the silver band, meant nothing to her. At length she placed the ring carefully upon her finger, and proceeded to cover it by putting on her glove.

For a long time she sat, speculating upon the strange workings of fate, which doomed her to be thus speeding alone to Brussels, instead of to Cherbourg, *en route* to America, with Richard by her side. The sight of two lovers, who boarded the train at St. Quentin, increased her dissatisfaction. They came into the compartment, evidently quite wrapped up in each other, and even the presence of a third person did not prevent them from holding each other's hands under the cover of a friendly magazine, and gazing at each other with longing eyes. Grace was quite unable to endure the sight of their happiness—she turned away and buried herself in her thoughts.

Presently the adventure-loving side of her nature began to assert itself. Richard had been sent on a mission of the greatest importance—one involving, Monsieur Lefevre had told her, the honor of both his country and himself. And she was to share it—to take part in its excitement, its dangers. The thought stirred all her love of the mysterious, the unusual. After all, since she had become the wife of a man whose profession in life was the detection of crime, should she not herself take an interest, an active part in his work, and thereby encourage and assist him? The thought made her impatient of all delay—she felt herself almost trying to urge the train to quicker motion—she was glad when at last they roared into the station at Brussels.

Grace had never before been in the Belgian capital, but she summoned a cab, and proceeded without difficulty to the Hotel Metropole. Here she was assigned to a small suite, and at once began to unpack the steamer trunk which was the only baggage she had brought with her. It was after four o'clock when she had completed this task, and had removed the stains of travel and changed her gown. As she came into the tiny parlor which formed the second of the two rooms of the suite, she heard a tapping at the door, and upon opening it, discovered one of the hotel maids, waiting outside with fresh towels. The girl came in, and busied herself setting to rights the toilet articles on the washstand. Grace, who was engaged in listlessly watching the traffic in the square outside, paid no attention to her. Presently she heard the girl come in from the bedroom, and inquire if there was anything else that she could do for her. "Nothing," she replied, without turning. The maid, however, did not leave the room, but stood near by, observing her. Grace faced about. "That is all," she said sharply.

"I have something to say to you, mademoiselle," the girl whispered in a low tone, as she took a step forward. "A message from Monsieur Lefevre."

"Monsieur Lefevre? You?"

"Yes, mademoiselle, I am in his confidence. I know the purpose of your visit here, and I come to give you further instructions." She spoke quietly, impressively, and Grace was convinced that she was what she represented herself to be. Still, she felt the necessity of caution. "Please explain," she remarked, without further committing herself.

The girl approached still closer, and reaching into the bosom of her dress, drew out a ring similar to the one which the Prefect had given Grace. It was attached to a bit of ribbon. She glanced at the ring on Grace's finger and smiled. "May I suggest, mademoiselle," she said, "that you place the ring you are wearing where it will be less conspicuous?"

Grace colored slightly at the criticism which the woman's words implied, but drew the ring from her finger and placed it in her purse. "What have you to say to me?" she inquired.

"This, mademoiselle. Certain persons, whose identity is not known to the police, have committed a theft in London—in fact, have stolen a valuable article from the

French Ambassador there, Monsieur de Grissac. This theft was committed this morning."

"What did they steal?" asked Grace.

"Monsieur de Grissac's ivory snuff box, mademoiselle."

"His snuff box? You don't mean to say that they are making all this fuss over a trifling thing like a snuff box?"

"Yes, mademoiselle. Such is, indeed, the case."

"But why?"

"That I cannot tell. I do not know. It is sufficient to me that Monsieur Lefevre wishes it recovered. In our service, mademoiselle, we are not supposed to ask questions, but to obey orders."

Grace repressed her annoyance as best she could. "I suppose it must be very valuable," she remarked, lamely.

"Undoubtedly. Very valuable, as you say. Now that it is stolen, it must be recovered without delay. Monsieur Lefevre informs us here in Brussels that others have gone to London to recover it. Should they fail to do so—we believe that the persons who have committed the theft will come here."

"Why?"

"Because they are acting, we believe, in the interests of a certain Dr. Hartmann, who is a resident of Brussels."

"Why should this Dr. Hartmann want the box?" asked Grace, somewhat mystified.

"That I am unable to tell you. He is an enemy of my country. He has many agents, and is a man of great power."

"But why don't you arrest him?"

"Alas, mademoiselle, you do not understand. This Dr. Hartmann is a physician of great prominence. His cures of nervous and mental disorders have made him famous throughout Europe. He has in Brussels—just outside the city, a sanatorium, where he receives and treats his patients. He is looked up to by all. His work as an enemy of France is quite secret, known to but a few. Even we know very little about it."

"Then how do you know that he had anything to do with the matter of this snuff box?"

"We do not know it—we only surmise. There is a reason, which I am not permitted at present to tell you, which causes Monsieur Lefevre to believe that Dr. Hartmann had a hand in this matter. It is for that reason, indeed, that he has sent you here."

"What can I do?"

"I will tell you. For a long time we have tried to get one of our own agents into Dr. Hartmann's house, but without success. He is very shrewd—very cautious. All his servants are countrymen of his, upon whom he knows he can depend. His patients are people of wealth, position, standing, who, he knows, could not possibly be agents of the French police. He will take no others, and always insists upon the strictest references. It is for these reasons that we have failed. Now an opportunity presents itself for you, mademoiselle, to accomplish that which the police cannot accomplish. You are an American girl, of prominent family, of wealth, of position. I am informed that your aunt, by her second marriage, was the Countess d'Este. Should you apply to Dr. Hartmann for treatment, you will have no difficulty in obtaining admission, for he could not, by any chance, think that Miss Grace Ellicott, of New York, was in the employ of the French secret police. You observe, mademoiselle, Monsieur the Prefect's object in sending you to Brussels?"

Grace nodded. She was beginning to feel a keen interest in the matter. "But I am not ill," she said, with a laugh. "How can I ask Dr. Hartmann to treat me?"

"We have thought of that. The matter has been under consideration ever since we were advised, early this afternoon, that you were coming. We have thought it best that you represent yourself to the doctor as a somnambulist."

"A sleep walker?"

"Precisely. It is a form of nervous trouble which is by no means infrequent. We are informed that Dr.

Hartmann has treated several such cases in the past. There are not symptoms, except a state of nervousness on the part of the patient which in your case it is probable the excitement of the enterprise will supply, and, of course, the tendency to walking in the sleep. This latter you must assume."

"Assume?"

"Yes. You must pretend to be a somnambulist. You must get up, each night, at some hour, and wander about the house—pretending to be oblivious of all about you. You are not normally conscious. You are in a walking dream. Your eyes are fixed ahead—seeing no one. It will not be difficult for you to pretend all this—and naturally, by wandering about in this way, you may—we hope you will—have excellent opportunities to observe what goes on within the doctor's walls."

"Is that all I am to do—just watch?"

"I think not. If we are unable, by other means, to prevent the stolen box from being delivered to Dr. Hartmann, it must be recovered from him, at any cost— at any cost whatever—" the woman repeated, significantly. "Even life itself cannot be spared, in this case. The box *must be recovered*, no matter what the price we pay—so we are informed by Monsieur Lefevre."

"Then if it should pass into his possession, I may have to steal it? Is that what you mean?"

"Undoubtedly, and at the very first opportunity." The girl rose, gathered up the soiled towels which she had taken from the bedroom, and went toward the door. "That is all, mademoiselle, except that you will communicate to us any news of importance by means of a young man who goes to the house each morning and evening to deliver bread. He comes in a small wagon, and you will no doubt be able to speak with him, as he enters or leaves the grounds. He is quite safe, and can be trusted. Address your communications to him verbally—no letters, understand; they are always dangerous. And now, let me suggest that you arrange to see Dr. Hartmann at once."

"But—he may require reference—credentials."

"We have thought of that, and have prepared the way. One of our men has ascertained that the United States Minister here is acquainted with you—that your family is known to him. Your aunt, you will remember, was quite prominent in society, in New York, at the time she married Monsieur the Count d'Este. Whether the Minister is acquainted with you personally, we have not been able to learn, but that he knows who you are, is certain."

"Then I had best call upon him, and arrange for letters to Dr. Hartmann."

"That is the best course. His house is near by. Take a cab at once, go to him, and state your errand. You will have no difficulty, I feel sure." She noiselessly opened the door, and in a moment was gone, leaving Grace in a state of wonder. She did not waste much time, however, in speculating upon the curious affair in which she found herself involved, but putting on her hat, started off at once in search of the American Minister.

CHAPTER III

When Richard Duvall and his companion entered the house of the French Ambassador in London, it was evident that their arrival was expected. The detective had no more than given his name to the butler who threw open the door, when the latter, with a bow of recognition, conducted them to a small reception-room to the right of the entrance, and informed them that Monsieur de Grissac would see them at once.

They did not have long to wait. The Ambassador, a thin, spare, nervous-looking man of sixty, with white hair and a gray-white mustache, came hurriedly into the room after but a few moments had elapsed, and greeting them excitedly, bade them be seated. He himself remained standing, his back to the fireplace, twirling his eyeglasses at the end of their black silk ribbon, and observing his visitors keenly.

"Monsieur Lefevre had informed me of your coming, gentlemen," he presently burst out. "We have no time to lose."

"Let us have the details of the affair, monsieur." Duvall remarked, seating himself comfortably in his chair. "So far we are completely in the dark."

"You know, do you not, that a valuable article, a small snuff box, to be exact—has been stolen from me?"

"Yes. Of that I have been informed," the detective remarked, dryly. "I am curious to learn why the loss of an article of so trivial a nature should be regarded with such seriousness."

The Ambassador's eyes snapped—he seemed almost to resent the detective's attitude. "It should be sufficient, monsieur, I think, that it is so regarded. The task before us is to recover it—not discuss the reasons for doing so."

"I disagree with you, monsieur. If the real value of the stolen article is kept from me, how can I draw any conclusions as to the probable object of its theft? Was it intrinsically valuable? Did it contain anything of value? In short, why should any one have taken the trouble to steal it? Tell me that, and I can act intelligently. Otherwise, I shall be only groping about in the dark."

"I do not think so, monsieur." The Ambassador bent upon Duvall a searching glance. "The fact that the box is gone should be sufficient. All that I ask is that you recover it. You must trace its disappearance from the material facts of the case. Conjecture will avail us nothing."

"Is the box then of no value?"

"I have not said so. As a matter of fact, its value is great. It has been an heirloom in my family for many years. At one time it belonged to Cardinal Mazarin."

"You think, then, that its intrinsic value alone might have prompted the theft?"

"I think so—indeed, I very greatly hope so."

"Why?"

The Ambassador recovered himself with a start. Evidently he had said more than he intended. It was some time before he answered the question and then he did so lamely. "Its theft by someone interested in its value as a curiosity would enable me to recover it most readily—by the payment, of course, of a sum of money."

"True. But I assume, from what you say, that there might be other reasons; that it might have been taken by those who suspected that it had another value?"

For a moment Monsieur de Grissac appeared confused. Then he waved his hand impatiently. "There are those," he said, "who seek to injure me. They know that I prized this thing highly. Their motive may have been—not money, but revenge. In that case, its recovery will be vastly more difficult."

Duvall saw that Monsieur de Grissac was not being frank with him, and for a moment he was conscious of a deep sense of annoyance. Monsieur Lefevre had, heretofore, invariably taken him into his confidence. He controlled his feelings, however, and appeared to be satisfied with the Ambassador's explanations. "What did the box contain, Monsieur de Grissac," he asked, pleasantly.

"A quantity of snuff, monsieur."

"Nothing else?"

"Nothing."

"Oh! And you, monsieur, are in the habit of using snuff?"

"Yes. It is the only form in which I use tobacco. Old-fashioned, perhaps, but I belong to the older generation." He straightened himself up suddenly. "Let us proceed, gentlemen. I fear we are wasting valuable time."

Duvall nodded. "Permit me to ask you a few more questions."

"I am at your service, monsieur."

"When did you last see the box?"

"This morning, at nine o'clock. I always carry it in the right-hand pocket of my waistcoat. To insure its safety, I had it attached to a long gold chain, which was securely fastened to the inside of the pocket. I rose this morning somewhat late, having attended a banquet last night. After having my coffee and rolls in my bedroom, I went to my dressing-room to be shaved. As I did so, I paused for a moment, drew the snuff box from the pocket of my white evening waistcoat, which my valet had hung in a closet the night before, and took a pinch of snuff from it. I then replaced it in the pocket and entered the dressing-room adjoining, where Noel, my man, was waiting for me. He proceeded to shave me as usual, and I began to dress. Upon going to the closet in my bedroom to remove the box, and fasten it by means of the chain to the clasp in the pocket of the waistcoat I had just put on, I was amazed to find it gone. I at once summoned Noel—"

"Summoned him?" interrupted the detective. "Was he not with you in the room?"

"No. A few moments before—as soon, in fact, as I had completed dressing, he left the apartment to give some instructions to my chauffeur."

"What did you do then?"

"I at once rushed out into the hall, calling for Noel."

"You believed, then, that he had taken the box?"

"I could believe nothing else. No one but he had been in my rooms."

"Oh! I see. And you questioned him?"

"Yes. On reaching the hall I met one of the maids ascending the stairway. I called to her, asking if she had seen Noel. She had not. She had been in the servants' hall—talking with the chauffeur—Noel had not been there."

"What did you do then?"

"I rushed to his room, which is on the floor above, thinking that, if he had taken the box, and proposed to deny the fact, he would have gone there to secrete it."

"Would he not have been more likely to leave the house immediately since he knew you would discover your loss at once?"

"No. He would realize that to flee would be to admit his guilt. He could not have gone more than a few hundred feet. Capture would have been inevitable."

"Did you find the man in the room?"

"He was just leaving it as I came up."

"What did you do then?"

"I ordered him back into the room, and questioned him sharply. He denied all knowledge of the matter, and appeared to be deeply hurt at my suspicions."

"Did you believe him?"

"I do not know. The matter is incomprehensible. Noel has been in my service for eight years. I supposed him absolutely incorruptible—absolutely honest. He also insists that after I left the bedroom, and came into the dressing-room to be shaved, he did not leave me, nor again enter the bedroom; in which case, he could not have committed the theft."

"Is this true?"

"So far as I can remember, it is." He spoke in a slightly hesitating way, and Duvall at once noticed it. "You are, then, not absolutely sure?" he asked.

"I feel confident that Noel did not leave me, nor enter the bedroom. If I hesitated for a moment, it arose from the fact that on one or two occasions I have fallen asleep while being shaved, but this morning I am quite sure that I did not do so."

"Yet you were up late last night, and awoke feeling sleepy and tired."

"Yes." The Ambassador nodded. "That is true."

"Is there any other door to the bedroom?"

"None, except that which opens into my bath. The bathroom has no windows. It is an inside room."

"And the bedroom?"

"It has two windows, facing upon the adjoining property. There is quite thirty feet of space between the two buildings and the windows are at least twenty-five feet from the ground."

"What room is above?"

"A guest's chamber, unused and locked."

Duvall rose and began to stride up and down the room, chewing viciously upon his unlighted cigar. "After you finished questioning the man, what did you do then?"

"I searched his room thoroughly, and made him turn out the contents of his pockets, his trunk and bureau drawers."

"And you found—?"

"Nothing. That was before noon to-day. Since then, I have kept the man locked in his room, awaiting your coming. One of the other servants has remained on guard outside his door ever since."

"You did not, then, notify the police?"

"No. The matter is one that, for reasons of my own, I do not wish to become public."

"Has anything been heard from your prisoner since this morning?"

"Yes. He asked for pen and ink about one o'clock this afternoon. I went up to see him, to find out why he wanted them. He seemed deeply affected, was almost in tears, and apparently afraid to meet my gaze. He said he wished to write a note, breaking an engagement he had had for this afternoon. He usually had Wednesday afternoons off. I permitted him to write the letter."

Duvall began to show signs of deep interest on hearing this. "Where is it?" he exclaimed.

"What, monsieur?" The Ambassador evidently did not follow him.

"The letter."

"I sent it, of course."

"But you read it first?"

"Yes. It was addressed to a man named Seltz, Oscar Seltz, if I recollect correctly, at a barber shop in Piccadilly Circus, which, as you know, is close by. This fellow Seltz was a friend of Noel's. I have several times heard him speak of him. They were accustomed to spend their afternoons off together, I understand."

"And the note?" asked Duvall, impatiently. "What did it say?"

"Merely that Noel was unable to keep his appointment for that afternoon, and did not expect to see his friend again before his departure. Seltz must have been planning some trip. The letter, as I remember, was quite cool, almost unfriendly in its tone."

Duvall glanced at his watch. "This was about one o'clock you say?"

"Yes. The matter has no significance. We are wasting our time discussing it."

"On the contrary, monsieur, I fear it may have had the greatest significance. That letter should never have been delivered. Even now, it may be too late to prevent the consequences. Be so good, monsieur, as to conduct me to this man Noel's room at once." He turned to Dufrenne. "You will accompany us, of course, Monsieur Dufrenne," he said, then followed the Ambassador toward the hall.

In a few moments they reached the third floor of the house, and passed along a short hall which gave entrance to a rear extension of the building, in which the servants' quarters were located. At the entrance of the hall, a maid was seated upon a stool, reading a book. She rose as the others approached, and stood respectfully aside.

"Has anything been heard from Noel?" the Ambassador asked. "Has he asked for anything?"

"Nothing, monsieur. He has been quiet ever since six o'clock, when I took him his supper."

"What was he doing when you entered?"

"Writing, monsieur. He was sitting at the table, with a pen in his hand, and he looked up and told me to put the tray on the trunk. 'I shall ask you to take this letter to Monsieur de Grissac as soon as I have finished it,' he said. Since then I have heard nothing from him."

Duvall had preceded the Ambassador and Dufrenne to the door at the end of the short hall, and stood listening intently. In a moment, De Grissac came up, and, unlocking the door, threw it open. The room was dimly illuminated by a single candle, which smoked and guttered in its socket, apparently nearly burned out. Nothing was at first to be seen of the valet. Duvall stepped forward, then turned quickly and spoke. "Shut the door, please," he said in a tense voice.

Dufrenne did so, while the Ambassador strode forward and followed Duvall's gaze with a look of horror. On the floor beside the bed, and to the far side of the room from the door, lay the body of the unfortunate valet, his face, ghastly pale, turned toward the ceiling. But it was neither the sight of the man lying there, apparently dead, nor the agonized expression of his face, which caused both the Ambassador and Duvall to start back with exclamations of surprise. Across the man's lips was a great, dull-red blotch, which at first appeared to be a clot of blood, but which seemed, from its circular form and regular contour, more like a huge seal. And seal it was. Duvall, dropping on one knee beside the body, felt for the man's heart, at the same time looking closely at the mark upon his lips. He was quite dead, and had apparently been so for an hour or two. The blot upon his face was a great lump of red sealing wax, tightly binding together his lips, and upon it was the coarse imprint of a man's forefingers.

The Ambassador shrank back with a cry, as his eyes fell upon the ghastly sight. Dufrenne gazed at the dead man impassively. Duvall, springing to his feet, went at once to the window at the rear of the room, which stood partly open, and raising it to its full extent, looked out. The others heard him give utterance to a low whistle, as he drew back into the room.

"No one could have entered the room," cried the Ambassador, in a frightened voice. "It is thirty-five feet or more to the ground."

Duvall motioned to the window. "Look out, monsieur," he remarked, quietly.

De Grissac did so, then uttered a sudden cry. From the window to the garden below stretched a long slender wooden ladder. "It belongs to the men who have been repairing the rain spouting," he exclaimed. "They leave it in the garden, at night. I knew there was no way in which Noel could get out."

"But clearly a way, monsieur, by which others could get in," said Duvall, quietly, as he began a minute examination of the room.

"But the snuff box—do you think it has been taken away?"

"Undoubtedly, monsieur. I suspected as much, when you showed me the man's letter. Your servant, I have no doubt, took the box while shaving you this morning. You doubtless dozed off, thus giving him the opportunity. He did not know that you had taken snuff from the box this morning shortly after arising, and imagined, no doubt, that you would suppose you had lost it some time the night before. This would relieve him of any suspicion. He hurried off to his room to secrete the box, meaning to deliver it to this friend of his, Oscar Seltz, during the afternoon. His arraignment by you, his subsequent imprisonment, no doubt frightened him and filled him with remorse—hence his rather unfriendly letter to Seltz. He had repented of his bargain, and was doubtless engaged in preparing a confession, telling you of his crime, and the reasons therefor, when the murderer entered the room.

"The latter, who probably was this man Seltz, must have become alarmed by the tone of Noel's letter. He was, it seems clear, planning some trip away from London, upon which he was about to leave. He meant to take the snuff box with him. Upon receiving Noel's letter he determined to see him and demand the box, if he found the latter had secured it. No doubt he made inquiries from some of the servants, on calling to see Noel, and was informed that he was confined to his room. He then pretended to leave, but in reality, ascended to the room by means of the ladder he found in the garden, while the servants were at dinner. It was a desperate chance, but he took it. Upon arriving in the room, he found Noel engaged in preparing his confession, insisted upon reading it, then realizing that his confederate was about to play him false, killed him, after gaining possession of the box, and departed."

The Ambassador uttered a groan. "My God," he moaned, "I am lost!"

Dufrenne, who meanwhile had been making a careful examination of the dead valet's body, rose with a mystified expression upon his face. "There are no wounds upon the body at all, Monsieur Duvall," he said. "How can you account for this man's death?"

Duvall stooped, and repeated the examination which his companion had just made. "You are right," he said. "The case is a most mysterious one."

"At least we can identify the murderer by the finger print upon the seal," De Grissac remarked, eagerly.

"I'm afraid not. This man Seltz cannot be quite a fool. Look!" He held up the forefinger of the dead man's right hand, upon which was a dull red burn, with bits of the red sealing wax about the nail. "He wasn't taking any chances." He let the already stiffening arm fall, and continued his examination of the body. "The method by which the man was killed," he remarked slowly, "is not yet clear to me. Certain finger prints on the throat indicate that he might have been strangled, but they are hardly deep or extensive enough for that. I fancy they would have resulted in temporary unconsciousness only. No—there is another reason—although what it is—" He paused as his eyes lit upon a thin shining object on the floor beside the table. "Oh, this may tell us something." He picked up the thing, which the others saw at once to be a large scarf pin, and examined it carefully.

"Did this belong to your servant, Monsieur de Grissac," he asked, holding the pin up to the light.

"Yes." The Ambassador glanced at the pin carelessly. "It was one of my own that I had given him, some months ago."

Duvall laid the scarf pin carefully upon the table, then went to the body on the floor, turned it over and made a careful examination of the back of the neck. He held the candle close, pushing aside the man's thin sandy hair. Presently he rose and placed the candle on the table beside the pin. "This was what your servant was killed with, Monsieur de Grissac," he said, as he indicated the scarf pin with his finger. "It was thrust violently into the spine, at the base of the brain. Only a tiny blood spot remains to tell the tale. This fellow Seltz is a shrewd customer."

"We do not even know that it was he who committed the crime. There is no real evidence against anyone. The snuff box may still be here. I insist that you make a thorough search."

"It would be useless, monsieur," Duvall remarked with a faint smile. "The box must have been on the table when the murderer entered the room."

"Why?"

"Because otherwise he would have searched for it, and you would have found everything in disorder. Believe me, monsieur, your servant had repented of his theft, and was about to return the box to you—it was that which caused his death. The seal upon his lips is a gruesome joke— silence—his lips are sealed—he can tell nothing."

"Seltz must be arrested at once," the Ambassador cried, in a rage.

"So far, monsieur, there is not the slightest evidence against him. Further, it is my opinion that he will leave London at once. Tell me the name of the shop in Piccadilly Circus where he was employed, and we will lose no further time in getting on his trail."

The Ambassador was not entirely certain of the location of the shop. He had never visited it. The name, he remembered, was given in the note as Perrier. The note had been delivered by one of the servants; he could tell where, and to whom he had delivered it.

Duvall recommended to the Ambassador that he report the murder to the police at once, but requested that no mention be made of the presence of himself and Monsieur Dufrenne. "We should be held as witnesses," he cautioned Monsieur de Grissac, "and that would seriously interfere with our plans. Let us interview the servant who took the letter at once."

The latter, a groom, was soon disposed of. He gave the number and location of the barber shop in Piccadilly Circus, a short distance away, and reported that he had handed the message to a dark, smooth-shaven man at the second chair. He did not know Seltz, but the proprietor had pointed him out in response to his inquiries. His description of the man was vague and unsatisfactory; he was unable to give any further information on the subject. Investigations as to anyone having made inquiries at the servants' entrance during the evening, regarding Noel, elicited the information that a heavily built, dark man, smooth-shaven, had called about half-past seven, and upon being informed that the valet was confined to his room and could not be seen, had disappeared. No one had taken any particular notice of his coming or going.

When the party had once more assembled in the reception-room, Duvall turned to Monsieur de Grissac. "There is nothing more to be accomplished here, monsieur," he remarked, quietly. "We will get after this fellow Seltz at once, and I trust that before long the missing snuff box will be returned to you."

The Ambassador shook hands with his guests, in a state of extreme agitation. "Lose no time," he urged. "You must recover the box before the thief has an opportunity to turn it over to those who are back of him, else it will be too late. I shall pray for your success." He stood at the door as his guests departed, shaking as though with a palsy. "It is a matter of greater moment than life itself. I trust you will not fail."

CHAPTER IV

Richard Duvall, accompanied by the silent little curio dealer, left the home of the French Ambassador and walked rapidly to the barber shop of Alphonse Perrier in Piccadilly Circus. They found the place without difficulty, a large and evidently prosperous establishment, located on the ground floor of a building, the upper rooms of which were devoted to business offices. A large plate glass window in front bore the sign, "Alphonse Perrier, Tonsorial Parlors."

The detective and his companion walked slowly past the brightly lighted window, their eyes taking in the details of the interior of the place. It was now close to ten o'clock, but the street was filled with pedestrians, and there were still one or two customers in the shop. At the first chair toward the door stood a large pasty-faced man, with a mop of bushy black hair, who was engaged in trimming a young man's mustache. The second chair was occupied by a man who was being shaved. The fellow who was shaving him answered in a general way to the descriptions of Seltz given by the Ambassador's servants. The third chair was unoccupied, and the man in charge of it, as well as those at the remaining two chairs, were engaged in putting away their razors and brushes, preparatory to leaving. It was evident that the closing hour was near at hand.

Duvall turned to his companion, "Monsieur Dufrenne," he said, "will you enter at once and take the third chair? Keep your eyes and ears open, and see what you can learn. I will wait here in the shadow of the next doorway. Our man is evidently inside. He will soon be leaving the shop. If he does so, before you do, I shall follow him. In that event, return to Monsieur de Grissac's house and wait there for word from me."

Dufrenne felt his stubbly beard. "It is fortunate, monsieur, that I have not been shaved since Monday," he said, as he entered the shop.

The man in charge of the third chair looked at him with a sulky expression as he took his seat. His companions grinned. Evidently he had not expected another customer before the closing hour. He began to shave the little old Frenchman with careless haste. The latter lay in his chair, with half-closed eyes, pretending to doze. In reality he was watching every movement of the man next to him.

The customer who occupied the second chair was a small, thin man, with sandy hair and a bony face. His eyes, rather prominent, under sparse red eyebrows, were closed as though in sleep. He was not paying the slightest attention to his surroundings, taking no notice whatever of Seltz, who was going over his face in a stolid and methodical way. There seemed nothing about either of them to attract attention—and Dufrenne began to wonder whether they might not after all be upon a false scent. The man Seltz showed neither haste nor nervousness in his movements—if he was in a hurry to finish his work for the evening, and leave the place, he certainly did not show it.

After a time, Dufrenne observed that the thin man in the chair next to him had opened his eyes, and was feeling his jaw with much satisfaction. "A very good shave, my good fellow," he said, in excellent English, without a trace of any foreign accent. "What powder was that you used, may I ask?"

Dufrenne, who was observing Seltz carelessly, saw a sudden change come over him. His eyes lit up with interest, and a slight flush overspread his face. There seemed nothing in so simple a question to arouse him in this way, and Dufrenne watched him carefully, his senses keenly alert for anything of interest. To his disappointment, Seltz's answer was of the most commonplace character. "It is a special kind, which Monsieur Perrier has made for him, after his own formula. 'Poudre Perrier,' it is called." He turned to the case behind him, opened a drawer and brought forth a round cardboard box. "Eightpence is the price. Would you like to try a box?" He extended the package toward his customer, who had risen and was adjusting his scarf at the mirror.

The man turned and glanced carelessly at the box. "Oh, you might wrap it up. I shave myself, occasionally, when I'm traveling. Eightpence, you say?"

"Yes, sir." Seltz turned to the case and began to do up the package in a piece of brown paper. In a few moments he turned and handed it to his customer, who had drawn on his coat, and was preparing to leave the place. Dufrenne saw him put his hand into his pocket and draw out some money, which he handed to Seltz. The latter nodded gravely and placed it in his pocket. The thin-faced man did the same with the package, then left the shop. There was nothing in the least suspicious about the whole transaction, and the little Frenchman contented himself with observing Seltz as he put away his brushes and prepared to stop work for the day. Once he saw the man draw something from his pocket and glance hurriedly at it, but his back was toward the chair in which Dufrenne sat, and he could not see what it was. A sense of uneasiness filled him, however, as the man who was shaving him drew away the sheet from about his shoulders and stepped back to allow him to rise.

He made his way to the street as quickly as possible. Seltz was still occupied in putting away his shaving implements.

On reaching the pavement, Dufrenne turned and walked rapidly toward Charing Cross. He did not wish to join Duvall in sight of those within. He had taken but a few paces when the latter caught up to him. "What did you learn?" the detective asked, quickly.

Dufrenne related in a few words what had occurred in the shop. He failed to note the excitement with which the detective listened to his story. "It may have been the snuff box," Duvall cried, moving forward rapidly in his excitement. "A clever scheme, I must say." He looked about eagerly for the man who had left the shop so short a time before, but he had disappeared in the darkness. "If you could only have warned me in some way."

"It was impossible, monsieur," said Dufrenne much crestfallen. "I could not leave the chair until the man had finished shaving me."

"Of course not," replied Duvall, uncertain what course to pursue next. "The man went in this direction. I noticed him particularly. Perhaps if I were to hurry I might overtake him." He started forward. "You stay here and watch Seltz. If I do not return, report to me at Monsieur de Grissac's." He turned and disappeared in the crowd.

Dufrenne went slowly back to the neighborhood of the shop, and stood in the shadow of the doorway, waiting. Presently he observed two of the assistants, in street clothes, leave the place and hurry off into the darkness. Neither of them was Seltz. The lights in the shop began to go out. Another assistant left. Only Seltz and the proprietor now remained within. He crept toward the window, and cautiously looked inside. Monsieur Perrier stood before one of the mirrors, arranging his bushy hair. *There was no one else in the shop.*

CHAPTER V

Grace Duvall arrived at the house of the American Minister at about half-past five, and luckily found him at home. From the maid at the hotel she had learned that his name was Phelps, Austin Phelps, and she at once recognized it as that of a lawyer prominent in business and social circles in New York. That he should know her, at least by name, was not at all surprising—her aunt, prior to her marriage to Count d'Este, had been much courted on account of both her beauty and her wealth. She waited in the handsome drawing-room to which she had been conducted, nervously wondering what the nature of her reception would be. The card she had given to the servant was one of her own—in fact, she remembered with a smile that her marriage to Richard Duvall but a few hours before had so filled her mind and heart that she had completely forgotten to have any cards prepared setting forth her new estate. It was as Grace Ellicott that the Minister would know her, however, and her business in Brussels made it desirable that she should pose as a single woman. It was not at all difficult, she thought to herself, under the circumstances.

Mr. Phelps, the Minister, proved to be a rubicund, rather portly gentleman, with white side whiskers and an air of urbane courtesy that set her at her ease at once. She told him who she was, hopefully, and was delighted to find that he placed her at once.

"Margaret Ellicott's niece," he said with a pleasant smile, offering his hand. "My dear girl, I'm delighted to meet you. I knew your aunt well, years ago, when you were going about in short dresses. I lost sight of her, after she married D'Este, and went to Paris to live. It was only the other day that I learned of her death. She was a fine woman. Mrs. Phelps and myself were both very fond of her. Won't you take a seat and tell me what you are doing in Brussels?"

Grace sat down, and at once plunged into her story. "I have suffered a great deal, lately, Mr. Phelps," she began, "from nervousness. I've been living in Paris, you know, and many things have happened to upset me. You have heard, of course, of the Count d'Este's treatment of me, and of his arrest and conviction?"

"Yes." He nodded gravely. "I do not wonder that you feel upset."

"Of late I have suffered a great deal from attacks of sleep walking. I get up at night and wander about, without knowing what I am doing. One night, I went out on the balcony and nearly walked off into the street." She lied bravely, hoping that her story would appear plausible.

"Too bad," Mr. Phelps remarked, evidently somewhat surprised that she should confide such matters to him. "You are under treatment, of course."

"No—that is, not at present. No one in Paris has been able to do me any good. I have heard so much of Dr. Hartmann and his marvelous success with all sorts of mental and nervous troubles that I have decided to consult him. That is why I came to Brussels."

"I see. Well—he's a splendid man. You couldn't do better. I know him very well, and like him immensely. A thorough scientist. Have you seen him, yet?"

"No. I—I understood that he does not care to take patients without references as to their standing, financial and otherwise."

"My dear girl, you would have no trouble. Of course he is overrun with patients—and as his sanatorium is a small one, he is obliged to charge large fees and take only the best and wealthiest class. He is an investigator, rather than a practitioner, and for that reason is obliged to guard his time."

"Then may I ask that you will give me a letter to him?" Grace said, hesitatingly.

"Certainly. I'll do it gladly. When do you intend to call on him?"

"I thought of going at once."

"Then I'll do better than give you a letter. I'll call him up by telephone and make an appointment for you. Say in half an hour. It will take you about twenty minutes to drive to his place. Will that be convenient?"

"Perfectly, Mr. Phelps, and thank you very much."

"Nonsense, my dear girl. Only too happy to do it for you. You must come and meet Mrs. Phelps, later on, and dine with us. Just at present she is out, taking tea with some friends. I want you to know her." He rose and started toward the door. "Excuse me for a few moments, while I telephone the doctor."

Grace, left alone, could not help regretting the deceit she had been obliged to practise upon her aunt's old friend, but there seemed to be no help for it. She only hoped that nothing would occur, subsequently, to involve the latter in any disagreeable explanations.

Mr. Phelps returned to the drawing-room in a few moments, his face weathed in smiles of satisfaction. "You're lucky," he said. "Dr. Hartmann tells me that he can accommodate you at once, as he discharged one of his patients, cured, only this morning. If you propose to remain at his house for treatment, which would be the only satisfactory way, I would suggest that you drive around by way of your hotel and arrange to have your baggage sent at once. I have written the address, and a few words to the doctor, on this card. Any of the cab drivers will know it, of course. Dr. Hartmann is one of the most prominent men in Brussels. I wish you good luck in your stay at his place, and whenever you are in the city, come in and have luncheon. Mrs. Phelps will be delighted." He led the way to the door, and ushered the girl into her cab. "Glad I was able to be of service to you," he said, as she drove off. "Good-evening."

When Grace entered the office of Dr. Hartmann, she was quite conscious of the fact that it would not be necessary for her to pretend to be nervous. In fact she felt herself turning hot and cold with fear, and wondered whether she would have the courage to play the part which had been so unexpectedly thrust upon her.

The place itself was pleasant and attractive enough in appearance. It consisted of a large stone building, with a mansard roof, set back some hundred or more yards from the street, and surrounded by a small park, filled with trees and shrubbery. A well-kept gravel driveway lead from the gate to the main entrance, which opened into a large hall. She observed as she came in, a sort of parlor, or reception-room, to the right, handsomely furnished in rather an old-fashioned style, with a large marble mantel and fireplace at one end of it. In the latter a blaze of cannel coal lit up the room with a pleasant radiance. It was not yet dark without, and the lights in the reception room were unlit, although a lamp was burning in the hall.

The maid who admitted her, a pleasant-faced German woman of middle age, conducted her into the reception-room, and taking her card, disappeared down the hall. In a few moments she returned, and nodding to Grace, opened a door at the left of the hall and bade her enter.

She found herself in the doctor's office, a large room, furnished in leather. A table in the center contained a lamp, and many magazines and papers. There was no one in the room when she entered, but before she had time to select a chair, a door at the rear of the room opened, and Dr. Hartmann came in.

He was a man of powerful build, and gave one the impression of great size, although not in reality above medium height. His shoulders, however, were very broad and thick, his neck short and powerful, his head large, with heavy iron-gray hair. A short beard of the same color covered the lower part of his face, while through a pair of gold-rimmed spectacles his eyes shone with piercing brightness. Grace thought, as he came toward her, that she had seldom seen a more striking-looking man.

"Be seated, miss," he said, addressing her in English, though with a decided accent. "You are Miss Grace Ellicott, I believe." He glanced at the card which he held in his hand.

"Yes," said Grace, nervously taking a seat.

"Mr. Phelps tells me you suffer from somnambulism,' the doctor went on. "How long have you observed the symptoms?"

"About six months," answered Grace, steadily.

"Are the occurrences frequent?"

"Yes. Almost every night."

"Had you experienced any great shock, about the time these manifestations began?"

"Yes. My aunt, whom I loved very dearly, had died."

"Oh! And when you walk in your sleep, do you seem to see her?"

Grace reflected over this question for several moments. Then she recollected that persons given to somnambulism never remember their experiences. "No. I have no recollection of what occurs."

The doctor's face was lit with a satisfied smile. He came over to Grace, drew apart the lids of one of her eyes and gazed into it, looked at her hands critically, felt her pulse for a moment, then asked suddenly, "Have you ever been placed under the influence of hypnosis?"

She trembled. If this man were to hypnotize her, as she was perfectly certain that he could, he might force her to tell him everything, and thereby endanger the success of the whole plan. "No," she replied, firmly. "I should not care for it."

"It is a method of treatment, miss, which I use a great deal."

"I hope it will not be necessary, doctor, to use it upon me. I have always had a horror of being hypnotized. Please do not attempt it."

"Very well, miss," the doctor laughed. "It may not be necessary. Before we go further with your case, I shall want to observe it carefully for a few days. You understand my terms, of course." The doctor named a large sum. "So much each week, and an additional charge for my services, depending upon the nature of the case."

Grace nodded, although the amount was sufficiently large to stagger her. "I shall gladly pay what you ask," she said, "if you can only cure me." She rose as the doctor stepped to the side of the room and pressed an electric button.

"You can go to your room at once, Miss Ellicott," the doctor went on. "One of the maids will conduct you. Your meals will be served there, or you can eat in the large dining-room, as you prefer. There are only twenty other patients. Some of them you might find very agreeable. Make yourself thoroughly at home. There are many excellent books in the library, and you will perhaps wish to walk in the grounds, or visit your friends in the city. The nature of your case is such that no particular regimen, no rules of health are necessary. Remember, however, that we close the gates of the park at sundown. I will see you again, this evening, and bring you some medicine. It is merely a sedative, to quiet your nerves. It is not possible to do much for complaints such as yours, by means of drugs." He turned, as a quiet, pleasant-faced woman opened the door. "Anna," he said to her in German, "conduct Miss Ellicott to her room, and make her comfortable."

Not wishing to endure the ordeal of dining with strangers, Grace decided to have her dinner served in her room. She found it excellent, and very well cooked. After dinner she sat in an easy chair by the large electric lamp and read a book she had brought with her.

At ten o'clock Dr. Hartmann came in, and asked her a few more questions, gave the nurse a small bottle containing a dark brown liquid and instructed her as to administering it, then said good-night and went out.

Grace threw down her book, and announced that she was ready to retire. The maid assisted her to undress, gave her a few drops of the medicine in a small glass of sherry, put out the light, and departed, informing Grace that she would be in the hall, within call, if the latter wished anything.

In spite of the medicine which she had taken, Grace was far too nervous and excited to fall asleep. She realized the daring nature of the game she had been called upon to play, and for a moment her spirits sank and she felt a sense of fear. Thoughts of Richard, however, soon restored her courage. She would face any danger to serve him. How different from what she had imagined, was this, her first night of married life! Instead of lying in Richard's arms, on board the steamer bound for America, here she was, a patient in a sanatorium in Brussels. The thing seemed unreal—impossible.

After a while, the noises of the house ceased one by one. As midnight struck, all was dark and silent. Only the faint sound of the wind among the trees in the park came to her ears. She wondered whether it was necessary for her to pretend to walk in her sleep this night—in order that the doctor might feel that her case was a real one. She rose softly, undecided, and going to the window, looked out.

The room in which she then was, occupied a position at the rear of the building, and in one of its two wings. From the center of the main building she observed a covered passageway, or bridge, extending out for perhaps a hundred feet and terminating in a sort of square tower. In one of the rooms in the tower, on a level with herself, she saw lights, and the figure of a man moving about.

The place attracted her attention. She wondered what its use could be. Then an inspiration struck her. The covered bridge ran from the main hall not thirty feet from her own door. She determined to cross it, pretending to be walking in her sleep, and find out what she could regarding the brick tower. When the time came, she knew that all the information she could possess about the house and its occupants would be necessary to the success of her plans.

She threw about her a dressing-gown, and quietly opened her door. The maid was nowhere to be seen, but doubtless she would shortly return. The chair upon which she had been sitting, at the point where the side and main halls met, stood directly beneath the electric light. No doubt, Grace thought, she had been called away for a few moments by one of the other patients on the floor.

Now was her chance. She stepped noiselessly down the cross hall, her eyes wide open and hands clenched at her sides. At the junction of the two halls she turned to the right, toward a door which, she judged, gave entrance to the covered way. She found this unlocked, opened it, entered the passageway and closed the door behind her. Then she began to walk slowly along the bridge.

It was a narrow structure, not exceeding five feet in width, with top and sides of corrugated metal, and a floor of wooden planks. At the far end of it she perceived a glass door, behind which shone a brilliant light.

She approached the door cautiously, keeping up all the while the pretense of walking in her sleep. This was not easy—she did not know just how persons who were somnambulists acted, but she had read descriptions of such cases, and had once seen a play in which one of the characters was a sleep walker. She tried to give her eyes a vacant, unseeing expression, and fearlessly approached the door.

It stood slightly ajar, and through the glass panels she saw at once that the room was Dr. Hartmann's laboratory. She arrived at this conclusion from the various medical appliances which stood about the room, the uses of which she did not know. Her inspection of the room, however, was but momentary, for two figures, brightly illuminated by an overhanging cluster of electric lights, at once attracted her attention. One of these was Dr. Hartmann. He sat at a large, flat-topped desk, his profile toward the door, examining with great care a mass of papers which lay on the desk before him. His forehead was wrinkled with thought, and an expression of anger dominated his face.

At the other side of the desk sat a tall spare man, with a military-looking carriage, and a fierce blond mustache, which he was gnawing uneasily. The two figures sat silent for several moments, no word passing between them, while Grace watched intently. Presently she heard the doctor speak. "It took you two years, it seems, to find out that Monsieur de Grissac uses snuff."

The other nodded. "One year and ten months, to be exact."

"And now," the doctor went on, angrily, "you trust everything to a stranger."

"It is better so, is it not? The affair is dangerous. Neither you, nor I, can afford to be mixed up in it."

Doctor Hartmann brought his fist down upon the desk with a bang. "*Gott in Himmel!*" he roared. "We must take some risks, my friend. I tell you I must have De Grissac's snuff box without further delay. If that does not solve the problem, we are at the end of our rope."

"It will solve it," the other man replied imperturbably. "I have positive assurances to that effect. Furthermore, I have every reason to believe that we shall hear from London before the end of the week."

"Have you received any word?" the doctor inquired eagerly.

"Yes. The attempt was to be made either to-day or to-morrow. Our man will report to you at once. He knows nothing of the matter, of course. He will deliver the box to you, and receive the money."

"Who is the fellow?"

"I do not know his name. I have not seen him, myself. Gratz arranged everything in London. I considered it very important that nothing should occur which would connect us with the matter in any way. Monsieur de Grissac will discover his loss very quickly and will use every effort to prevent the box from falling into our hands. Gratz and the others would invite suspicion at once. The fellow they have chosen to handle the matter is unknown to the French police. He will attract no attention. The plan appears to be perfect."

The doctor nodded slowly, chewing on his cigar. "I hope you are right, Mayer," he said, and looked at his watch.

As he finished speaking, Grace heard someone approaching her from behind, but she paid no attention. In a moment the attendant touched her lightly on the arm. She turned, gazing at the woman with staring, unseeing eyes. The latter looked at her keenly, then began to lead her along the bridge toward the main building.

When they reached her bedroom, the nurse turned on the lights suddenly, glancing at Grace's face as she did so. The girl did not dare even to blink her eyes. "Sit down," the woman commanded, sharply. Grace sank upon the edge of the bed. "Take off your shoes," the nurse went on, in a stern voice. The girl had slipped on a pair of bedroom slippers—she proceeded to remove them mechanically, fumbling with them as though trying to unfasten the laces of a pair of shoes. "Now your dress," the nurse ordered. Grace began awkwardly to remove the dressing-gown she had thrown about her. When the woman told her sharply to get into bed, she did so without a word, apparently quite unconscious of what she was doing. It was a splendid piece of acting, and she did it so well that if the nurse had any doubts as to the reality of her somnambulistic condition they were at once dispelled. As soon as the girl placed her head upon the pillows, she pretended to be sound asleep, her eyes closed, her breathing regular and slow. After a time, the attendant put out the light and left the room.

The girl lay still for hours, wondering what there was in the strange conversation she had overheard that could help Richard in his efforts to recover the stolen snuff box.

That it had been stolen she knew; that it had not yet been delivered to Dr. Hartmann she also knew. Perhaps Richard might have succeeded in recovering it before now; if not, the messenger bringing it to the doctor's office would undoubtedly arrive the next day. She determined to rise early, in order that she might, if possible, send word of what she had heard to Brussels by means of the young man who drove the delivery wagon.

CHAPTER VI

When Richard Duvall left Dufrenne, the curio dealer, in Piccadilly Circus, and started after the man who had purchased the box of powder in the barber shop, he realized to the full the hopelessness of his task. The man had left the shop at least two minutes before Dufrenne came out—perhaps more, and another minute had been consumed by the latter in telling his story. Three minutes' start, in a crowded street at night, was a handicap which the detective could scarcely hope to overcome.

He hurried along in the general direction the fellow had taken, trying to form in his mind a clear picture of his appearance. In the dim light before the shop he had not been able to observe him closely, nor had there, indeed, appeared any very good reason for doing so; he had thought the man but a belated customer of the place and had barely glanced at him.

His experience in summing up at a glance the general characteristics of those he met, however, stood him in good stead—he remembered that the man had worn a long brown overcoat, a derby hat, and carried in his hand a small satchel. The latter, which Dufrenne had failed to mention, indicated a traveler—the man's words to Seltz, on purchasing the box of powder, seemed to confirm it. The man had walked, apparently, instead of taking a cab. Charing Cross station was but a short distance away. What more natural, Duvall reasoned, than that the man he was following, was on his way to take a train?

Following this line of reasoning, the detective walked hastily in the direction of Charing Cross, dodging in and out among the passers-by, and eying keenly everyone he met, in the hope that he might discover the man with the satchel. He was, however, doomed to disappointment. After spending over fifteen minutes in Charing Cross station, watching the crowds at the booking offices, the telegraph and telephone booths and the restaurant, he concluded that he had been mistaken in his course of reasoning and reluctantly turned his steps once more toward the shop of M. Perrier. There was, of course, still the chance that his deductions had been wrong. Seltz might still have the snuff box in his possession, and the man with the satchel be merely a harmless individual who used rice powder after shaving. He almost reproached himself for having wasted so much time, and hurried along through Piccadilly Circus, in a state of considerable perplexity.

As he came up to the shop, he saw Dufrenne standing before the window, his eyes glued to the pane. Something in his astonished expression attracted the detective's attention at once. He tapped the curio dealer lightly on the shoulder.

Dufrenne turned suddenly, much startled, then recognizing Duvall, drew him to one side. "I have watched the door every minute since you left," he said in a trembling voice. "Seltz did not come out—yet he is not inside. No one is there but Monsieur Perrier."

Duvall started back with a muttered exclamation. "You—you must be mistaken," he cried.

"Look!" The Frenchman pointed to the window. Duvall glanced within. The proprietor of the place was its only occupant.

The detective turned to his companion and nodded. "Come inside," he said, shortly, and striding up to the door, threw it open and entered the place.

Monsieur Perrier, startled half out of his wits by the suddenness with which Duvall entered the room, dropped the comb with which he had been arranging his hair and turned with an alarmed face. "The shop—it is closed for the night," he said. "My men have all gone home."

"Has Seltz gone?" asked Duvall, sharply.

"Seltz? Surely. He left immediately after shaving this gentleman." Perrier indicated Dufrenne with a fat and trembling forefinger. "Is anything wrong, gentlemen? Was the shave not satisfactory?"

Duvall looked at the curio dealer with a smile of chagrin. "It's perfectly clear, Dufrenne," he said, somewhat crestfallen. "Our man went out as we were walking up the street—while you were telling me what happened in the shop."

The little old man nodded. Monsieur Perrier continued to gaze at his visitors. "What is it you wish, gentlemen?" he presently inquired.

"Where does Seltz live?" Duvall demanded, sharply.

"Alas—I do not know. He has worked for me but three months. I knew nothing of him—nothing at all. He—he asked for leave of absence yesterday—he was to be gone a week, but to-night he told me that he would not go."

Duvall's eyes lit up. He turned to Dufrenne. "After what happened—to-night," he said, significantly, "he feared to leave—thinking that his going away would be an admission of his guilt."

Again Dufrenne nodded. Monsieur Perrier looked at them with bulging eyes. "Guilt!" he exclaimed. "Has this fellow Seltz been doing anything he should not?"

"Possibly," Duvall ejaculated, dryly. "Do you happen to know where he was going?"

"He—he said something about visiting his parents. Oh—gentlemen—I beg of you, do not cause any scandal— it would ruin my trade. I shall discharge the fellow at once."

"You will do nothing of the sort," exclaimed Duvall, angrily. "If he reports for duty to-morrow, say nothing to him of our visit, or it will be worse for you." He leaned toward the terrified barber. "I am a detective," he said, shortly. "Be careful what you do."

Monsieur Perrier sank upon his knees, his hands lifted in supplication. "*Mon Dieu*—what shall I do—my business—it will be desolated—what shall I do?"

"Get up, and hold your tongue first of all. After that, tell me, if you can, where it was that Seltz intended to go, to visit his parents?"

"He spoke of Brussels—he intended to take the night boat from Harwich to Antwerp. I heard him discussing his plans with one of the other men."

"Brussels!" Duvall hurriedly glanced at his watch. "There's just time, if we hurry—come." He turned to Dufrenne, excitement showing in every line of his face. As he hurried toward the door he spoke over his shoulder to Monsieur Perrier. "Don't open your mouth to a soul—do you hear? If you do, you'll get yourself into a peck of trouble." The last thing they heard as they left the shop was the barber's howls of assent.

At the corner Duvall signaled a passing cab. "Liverpool Street station, in a hurry," he cried. "Half a crown extra, if you make the boat train for Harwich."

Dufrenne gazed at his companion in bewilderment. "I do not understand, Monsieur Duvall," he began, but the detective cut him short. "The thing is as plain as a pipe stem," he said. "Seltz expected to get the snuff box from the Ambassador's man this afternoon, and had made his arrangements to leave with it for Brussels at once. The events of the evening—culminating in Noel's murder, made him fear to do so. He realized that the note, delivered to him by one of the Ambassador's servants, might attract suspicion toward him, and therefore wisely made up his mind to remain quietly where he was, sending the box by some friend. He dared not hand the box to him at any place outside the shop, for fear he might be watched. No doubt he arranged with his friend to come to the place just before closing, and to pretend to buy the face powder, as you saw him do. Seltz had only to turn the powder out of the package, put the snuff box inside, and the thing was done. This he no doubt did at some opportune moment during the evening, when he was certain he was not observed. It is a mighty clever scheme—I'll admit. You saw nothing suspicious about the transaction, and I confess that I did not realize its significance at the time. Naturally the man to whom he gave the box will make for Brussels at once, since it was to that point that Seltz intended going. No doubt he was operating in the interests of someone else—some third person to whom the box is of great value, and who has agreed to pay a large sum for it on delivery. You saw the fellow who bought the powder hand Seltz money—how much you could not tell. It may be that Seltz was obliged to divide the reward with his friend, and that the latter has already turned over to Seltz his share in advance. Of that we cannot be certain, nor is it material. Seltz is undoubtedly guilty of the murder of the man Noel, but to stay here and arrest him now would only defeat the object we have in view. After the box has been recovered, we can return and deal with Seltz. You may be quite sure he will not dare to run away, for fear that by so doing he would admit his guilt."

Dufrenne looked at the detective in admiration. "You reason well, monsieur," he remarked. "But why should they be taking the box to Brussels?"

"That I cannot tell you, of course, except that, as I said before, the plot to steal it inevitably originated there. We shall learn more to-morrow, after we have arrived in the city. The next thing to be done is to find our man."

They arrived at Liverpool Street station just in time to swing aboard the train for Harwich as it was pulling out. There were not many passengers—they found themselves in a smoking-compartment quite to themselves.

"There is no use in attempting to do anything until we reach Harwich," the detective remarked, pulling his hat over his eyes. He leaned back and began to speculate disgustedly upon the events of the day. Married at noon— torn from his wife within an hour—in London at night—a murder—and now a wild chase to Brussels after a snuff box. It seemed almost ludicrous. He smiled grimly. He had not expected to spend in quite this way the first twelve hours of his honeymoon.

CHAPTER VII

On the morning of her first day at Dr. Hartmann's sanatorium, Grace Duvall rose early, and dressed herself for a walk. She was determined, if possible, to communicate the results of her adventure the night before to the French police in Brussels, and realizing that to do so by the only means in her power, namely, the young man who drove the delivery wagon, might involve considerable risk of discovery, she dressed herself as simply as possible, in a dark-gray suit and white shirtwaist.

She had her breakfast in her room, and then told the nurse that she intended to take a walk in the grounds. During breakfast she complained of the bread which was served her—and informed the maid that in her country people ate hot bread at breakfast. The woman seemed surprised. "Hot bread!" she exclaimed. "*Mon Dieu!* Who ever heard of such a thing."

"If you bake your bread here in the house," Grace went on, "you could easily serve hot bread or rolls to me."

"Impossible, mademoiselle. All our bread comes from a bakery in the city. A young man brings it each morning at ten o'clock."

Grace laughed inwardly. This was just the information for which she was seeking. It was then a little after nine. She felt tired and worn from her almost sleepless night, and her appearance showed it. When she told the nurse that she intended to take a stroll, and get some air, the latter nodded. "Dr. Hartmann has recommended it," she said. "He is a great believer in the value of fresh air." The woman made no reference to the events of the night before, nor did Grace. She knew that sleep walkers were not supposed to remember anything that occurred during their attacks of somnambulism.

On the way out she met Dr. Hartmann, returning from his after-breakfast constitutional. He was just entering his office. "Good morning, Miss Ellicott," he said, pleasantly. "May I ask you to step inside a moment? There are a few questions I should like to ask you."

She obeyed, much against her will. It was nearly half-past nine, she knew, and she must not miss the delivery man, if she was to send her message to Brussels. She heard the doctor saying that he would detain her but a few moments.

His first question sent the color to her cheeks, and she hesitated before answering it, realizing that it was a trap. "Do you feel any the worse, miss, from the experiences of last night?" he inquired.

For a moment she was about to say "no," but caught herself in time. "What experiences?" she asked, innocently enough. "Did I have an attack?"

She fancied that the doctor appeared relieved. He smiled as he replied. "You wandered about a little. The nurse must have been negligent. I have reprimanded her. You might readily have a serious accident, if left to yourself."

Grace looked at him with a smile which scarcely concealed her agitation. "I hope I caused no trouble," she said. "It is a frightful affliction. I trust you will be able to do something for me."

"Don't worry, my dear young lady. We shall cure you beyond a doubt. I think, however, that it will be necessary to employ hypnosis. All cases such as yours respond most readily to hypnotic suggestion. However, I shall observe your case for a while longer, before making a decision. You are going out for a walk, I see."

"Yes. I love the air." She rose with a secret fear of the man in her heart. If he should hypnotize her, what was there to prevent his learning everything. She determined to avoid this method of treatment at all costs, yet could not see how to do so without arousing his suspicions. "Good-morning," she said, hastily, as she left the room.

The walk to the entrance gate in the fresh autumn air served to revive her spirits wonderfully. Her original intention had been to stroll down the avenue which fronted the house, in the hope of meeting the delivery wagon on the way. In a moment the futility of this plan became apparent. She did not know from which direction the wagon would appear, nor would she be able to recognize it, even should she be lucky enough to meet it. She paused at the gate, uncertain, then began to walk along a path which led among the trees and shrubbery, with one eye all the while upon the gateway at the entrance. Once or twice vehicles passing along the road outside startled her into sudden action; she went toward the gate only to find that they had passed on. The tenseness of the situation began to get on her nerves; in her fear she was certain that she was being watched from the house, or by the gardener in the distance who was engaged in taking the leaves from the graveled walks. She had almost given up in despair when she heard the rumble of an approaching cart, and saw a smart little wagon driven by a young man in a blue jacket with large brass buttons, enter the gate.

She went quickly toward the roadway, pretending an interest in the horse. The young man saw her approaching, and looked at her shrewdly. She gave a slight nod, and continued to approach him. All of a sudden he threw down the reins, gave an exclamation, and jumping from the wagon, began to inspect the horse's feet with great deliberateness and care.

Grace went up to the horse, and began patting its nose. "Poor fellow," she said, consolingly, in English, looking all the while at the young man's face.

"Are you Miss Ellicott?" he said suddenly in rather halting English, without turning his head.

"Yes." Her reply was quick, eager. "Dr. Hartmann is expecting a messenger from London with the stolen snuff box to-day or to-morrow. I heard them talking about it, last night. The messenger is a stranger to him. He does not suspect that I am watching him."

The boy nodded gravely. "You are instructed to remain near the front of the house, or in the reception-room inside, as much as possible, during the day. The man from London is expected this morning. He may be here at any moment. Keep your eyes open." He began to whistle merrily, pretended to remove a stone from one of the horse's shoes, sprang back into the wagon and drove off to the house, without paying any further attention to her.

Grace walked slowly up the driveway, and finding a bench near a bed of geraniums, sat down and pretended to read a book which she had brought with her. After a time, the delivery wagon returned, but the boy did not even glance at her as he passed out. She noticed, however, that he was driving rapidly and appeared to be in a great hurry.

She sat on the bench for over an hour, wondering what would be the next development in this mysterious affair. She could not shake off the idea that she would soon see Richard, in spite of the fact that she had no definite reasons upon which to base her hopes. One thing, however, seemed certain. If the man with the stolen snuff box had arrived in Brussels, it clearly meant that Richard had failed to capture him in London, and it seemed not unreasonable to suppose that he would be following him.

She thought about the matter so much that it interfered with her attempts to read the book. After a while she closed it, and sat watching the distant gardener as he ceaselessly raked the gravel paths. Everything seemed so quiet, so full of peace—everything, in fact, but her own thoughts. Somehow it seemed impossible to believe that underneath all the beauty of this clear autumn day lay plotting, and tragedy, and even death.

It was close to noon, when she ceased her musings, and rising, went toward the house. Sitting so long in the open air had made her a bit chilly. She determined to seek the grateful warmth of the reception-room. As she mounted the steps of the house she heard sounds of a cab being driven rapidly along the main street, and a sudden intuition warned her that something of an unusual nature was about to happen. She glanced back, as the servant opened the door in response to her ring, and was not surprised to see that the vehicle had entered the grounds, and was rapidly approaching the house.

Her hasty glance showed her that it contained but a single occupant, a man, and in spite of the distance, she fancied that she detected something familiar about the poise of his head and shoulders. The thought was but momentary—she stepped at once into the reception-room at the right, sat down by the fire, and opening her book, pretended to be deeply absorbed in its contents. In reality she was observing narrowly the maid in the hallway, who stood at the open door, waiting to admit the man who was driving up in the cab.

CHAPTER VIII

When Richard Duvall and Dufrenne arrived at Harwich, on their way from London, the former requested his companion to turn up his coat collar, pull his soft hat over his eyes, and put on his spectacles. He feared that the man they were trying to locate might recognize the curio dealer as the person who had occupied the chair next to him in Monsieur Perrier's barber shop earlier in the evening. He also requested the Frenchman to make his way to the boat alone, keeping a sharp lookout for the man in the brown overcoat.

Duvall himself joined the straggling crowd of sleepy passengers as they went aboard the steamer for Antwerp, his eyes searching every passenger about him for some sight of the one he sought. Once he thought he recognized the man, a long way off, going up the steamer's gang plank, but he could not be sure, in the flickering light, that he was right.

He went aboard the boat, in some doubt as to whether, after all, his course of reasoning might not be incorrect. Here he was bound for the Continent, on the heels of a man whom he had no real proof was not at this moment sleeping peacefully in his bed in London.

The situation was a trying one. He lit a cigar and began to pace the deck nervously, inspecting the few passengers who had elected to remain outside, before directing his steps to the saloon below.

After some five minutes spent in a useless search, he observed a familiar figure approaching him from the direction of the companionway, and at once saw that it was Dufrenne. The latter passed him without any sign of recognition, but just as their elbows were almost touching, said in a low voice, "He is below, in the saloon, monsieur. Has not taken a stateroom."

Duvall continued his walk about the decks for a few moments longer, then threw away his cigar, and descended to the saloon. A number of passengers were dozing on the sofas, or in chairs, and at a table several were playing cards. He paused for a moment to watch the game, his eyes searching the room for the man in the brown overcoat. After a time he located him, sprawled in an easy chair, his eyes closed, his satchel tossed carelessly upon the floor beside him.

The detective began to stroll about the place, as though in deep thought. His eyes were fixed, however, upon the face of the man in the chair. It was a determined face, as the thin lips and close-set eyes showed, but Duvall noted with satisfaction signs of weakness about the half-open mouth. The man was undoubtedly sleeping soundly.

Duvall was at a loss to know just what to do. He was convinced that the ivory snuff box, upon the recovery of which Monsieur Lefevre had assured him the honor of France itself depended, was within ten feet of him, yet he could do nothing, apparently, at the moment, to regain it. To arrest the man, except on French soil, was out of the question. Even could he do so, the package which the latter had so carelessly slipped into his overcoat pocket in Monsieur Perrier's shop might contain, after all, but a harmless box of rice powder, and he would be hard put to explain satisfactorily his action. On the other hand, the presence of the snuff box on the man's person, supposing this to be beyond question, was not in itself sufficient to warrant placing him under arrest. He might claim it as his own property. There was nothing to show that it had been stolen. Clearly the only thing to do was to attempt to get the box from him by stealth.

After a long time spent in debating the matter pro and con, Duvall threw himself into a chair close to the one which the man he was watching occupied, and pretended to sleep. Of Dufrenne he saw nothing. After perhaps an hour, the card game ceased, the players retired to their staterooms, or to near-by sofas, and a steward began to lower the lights. Presently not a sound was to be heard throughout the saloon, except the chorus of snores from the sleeping passengers, and the creaking of the vessel as she plunged into the heavy Channel swell.

The detective slowly advanced his foot, and with infinite patience, began to draw toward him the small leather satchel which lay beside the man's chair. He did this so slowly and imperceptibly that the operation occupied the best part of a quarter of an hour. At last the bag was safely pushed beneath the folds of his overcoat, which he had removed on sitting down, and now lay thrown carelessly over his knees.

He bent over, noiselessly, his hand beneath the folds of the coat, and began to fumble with the catch of the satchel. In a few moments he managed to open it, and with nervous fingers examined the contents of the bag. Guided by the sense of touch only, he was able to identify successively a razor case, a shaving brush, a cotton nightshirt and a number of other articles of an ordinary and usual nature. He had almost given up the search, when his fingers closed about a small round object, done up in paper. His heart gave a leap of joy. He could feel the coarse string with which the package was bound and could tell from its lightness that it contained probably what he sought. In a moment he had drawn it noiselessly from the satchel and transferred it to the pocket of his coat.

The process of closing the bag and returning it to its former position was accomplished without waking the sleeping occupant of the near-by chair. Duvall was conscious of a feeling of exultation. He yawned, stretched himself, glanced with great deliberation at his watch, then rose and quietly left the room.

The decks seemed deserted. After some trouble he managed, however, to locate Dufrenne, standing beside the rail in the shadow of one of the lifeboats. He went up to him and saw that his teeth were chattering with the cold. Duvall could not repress a feeling of admiration for the little old Frenchman, who, rather than risk for a moment his identification by the man they were following, had elected to spend the night wandering about the decks. His patriotism was proof against even the cold.

Duvall touched him gently on the arm. "I have secured it," he remarked, quietly.

Dufrenne turned. "The snuff box?" he whispered excitedly.

The detective nodded, and cautiously drew the circular package from his pocket. "It was in his satchel," he remarked, as he began to remove the string.

Dufrenne's lips moved. He seemed to be offering up a silent prayer of thanks. He was scarcely able to contain his impatience as the detective slowly unwrapped the parcel, disclosing a small blue pasteboard box, on the cover of which, in black, appeared the words, "Poudre Perrier." In a moment Duvall had removed the lid, and plunged his finger into the box. As he did so, he uttered an exclamation of utter astonishment and disgust. The box contained nothing but rice powder.

CHAPTER IX

It would be difficult to describe the feelings of annoyance and chagrin which swept over Richard Duvall as he tossed the box of Monsieur Perrier's rice powder over the side of the vessel and watched it float for a moment on the crest of a wave before being swept into the darkness. He glanced for an instant at his companion, then turned away as he saw the latter's stare of astonishment and dismay. He wanted to be alone, to think out this matter for himself.

With a confusion of ideas racing through his brain he began to pace the deck, trying to discover wherein his reasoning had been at fault. He went back to the gruesome scene at the house of the Ambassador—the murdered valet, with the grim seal of silence upon his lips. Whoever had committed this murder had made away with the snuff box, of that he felt certain. Upon what, then, did his suspicions of Seltz rest? The evidence was slender—merely that the latter had had an appointment to meet the murdered man that afternoon, and that a person answering Seltz's description had inquired for the latter at the servants' entrance at Monsieur de Grissac's that evening. Not very convincing, surely, yet taken with Seltz's evident intention to leave London for Brussels that night, certainly significant. Following then his original hypothesis, that Seltz was the guilty man, and had the box in his possession, two solutions of the matter only seemed possible. The first was, the man in the saloon below, anticipating perhaps some attempt to search his baggage, had deliberately provided himself, through Seltz, with a second package, containing a box of rice powder only, which he had placed in his satchel, in the belief that, if found, its innocent contents would divert from him further suspicion. The careless way in which he had thrown his satchel on the floor beside him, favored this theory. It seemed, on sober thought, extremely unlikely that the bearer of so valuable a piece of property would be so thoughtless as to place it loosely in an unlocked handbag. Even now the real package might be reposing safely in some secure inner pocket.

The other solution was equally probable. The purchase of the face powder might have been quite innocent and *bona fide*. The man below might know nothing whatever about the snuff box, and Seltz might even now be on his way to Brussels to dispose of it, in accordance with his original intentions. If so, however, why had he informed Monsieur Perrier that he had changed his mind, and would not take the vacation he had requested? Was this merely a blind, to avert suspicion, in case the unexpected murder of the man Noel resulted in inquiries being made of Monsieur Perrier? Of course, when Seltz had spoken of his intention to go to Brussels, no thought of murder was in his mind—he had no vital object in hiding his movements—not having any reason to suppose that suspicion could possibly be attracted to him. After the sending of the note to him by Noel, he must have realized the danger of his position, and told Monsieur Perrier that his plans had changed, while in reality fully intending to carry them out as he had originally intended.

There was, of course, a possible third solution, namely, that Seltz had nothing to do with the murder at all, and was merely an innocent barber, quite unaware of all the mystery that was being woven about himself and his movements. In that event, as Duvall realized with the deepest chagrin, he would be obliged to return to London, and begin his investigations all over again. In this event, there could be but one starting point—the murder of the valet. Yet his painstaking examination of the scene of the murder had shown an utter absence of any clues. Even the weapon which had caused the valet's death was his own property—the finger print on the seal which closed his lips made with his own forefinger. And here the detective began to feel a deep sense of doubt as to the accuracy of his conclusions regarding Seltz's guilt. Would a man of his type have taken the trouble to place the gruesome seal upon the dead man's lips? This seemed, on second thoughts, the act of a hardened and unfeeling criminal—a man to whom murder was a scientific accomplishment, not a hasty and hideous crime. Was Seltz such a man? There was no answer to this question—the fleeting glimpses which Duvall had secured of his face, through the barber-shop window, had told him little or nothing of the man's character.

One fact, however, presently forced itself upon the detective's mind. If Seltz had left the shop for Brussels that night, according to his original intention, he must be somewhere on the boat. No night route from London to Belgium existed, except that by way of Harwich. He blamed himself that in his eagerness to discover the stranger with the satchel he had not thought to look for Seltz.

Upon the conclusion of his deliberations, Duvall crossed over to the other side of the boat, where he had left Dufrenne. The little old Frenchman stood gazing down at the sea, his face blue with cold, and filled with a look of bitter disappointment. He did not even glance up, as Duvall joined him.

"Come, Monsieur Dufrenne," the detective said, kindly. 'Let us go below."

The old man accompanied him without a word. As they reached the companionway, however, he spoke. "We must return to London at once," he said. "This same boat will take us back to Harwich."

"Yes," Duvall agreed, "unless we discover that Seltz is aboard."

"Seltz?" The Frenchman looked up, puzzled, yet with an expression of renewed hope in his eyes.

"Yes. We have apparently followed the wrong man. In that case, why not search for the right one. If Seltz is on board, we will follow him to Brussels. If not, we will return to London. We can make sure, when the passengers are discharged at Antwerp."

Dufrenne nodded eagerly. "It may indeed be possible," he remarked, as they entered the saloon.

Most of the passengers were on deck when the steamer reached her wharf at Antwerp, but in spite of a careful search, Duvall was unable to locate Seltz amongst them. He stood by the gang plank, watching the crowd as it left the boat, his eyes searching restlessly for the swarthy countenance of the barber. He had almost given up hope, when he saw a belated passenger hurriedly cross the deck and dart up the gang plank. He moved rapidly, his throat muffled in a blue neckcloth, his slouch hat pulled down over his eyes, but the glance which Duvall obtained of his somewhat scared face told him at once that he had located his man.

He signaled quietly to Dufrenne, who had been standing discreetly in the background for fear the barber might recognize him, and the two left the boat together, some forty or more yards in Seltz's rear.

They did not make any attempt to follow him closely. There seemed no room for doubt that he was bound for the train to Brussels, and Duvall and his companion followed along at a leisurely pace, showing nothing of the agitation they so keenly felt.

They purposely avoided any attempt to enter the same compartment with the barber, being satisfied when they saw him climb aboard the train. They did, however, watch the departing passengers at all stops, and when they rolled into the station at Brussels, they were certain that their man was aboard. Nor were they mistaken. They saw him alight, look swiftly about as though fearing that he was being followed, and then start at a rapid pace toward the street.

Duvall went after him at once, directing Dufrenne to go to the Hotel Metropole and secure a room in his own name, where he was to wait until he heard from his companion. These instructions given, the detective began to follow Seltz up the street.

The man evidently knew the town well. He made no pauses, and did not hesitate at any time during his long walk. It terminated at a small, third-class hotel in the older part of the city, where he went in, entered the cafe, and selecting a table in a dim corner, ordered breakfast.

Duvall, feeling safe in leaving him, at once sought a telephone and proceeded to call up Dufrenne at the Hotel Metropole.

The latter, meanwhile, had turned from the railway station, and was proceeding up the street at a leisurely pace, when a young man approached him from behind, and touched him lightly on the shoulder. "Monsieur Dufrenne?" he inquired, smiling.

The curio dealer glanced at the man who had accosted him, and an answering smile lit up his face. "Oh, Lablanche, glad to see you," he said. "I did not know you were on this case."

"Monsieur Lefevre sent me from Paris last night. We are expecting news at any moment. Monsieur Duvall is with you, I observe."

"Yes. He is following the man from London. He will telephone me, as soon as he learns his destination."

The man whom Dufrenne had addressed as Lablanche, looked grave. "This affair has, we believe, been engineered by a physician here—Dr. Hartmann— you have heard of him, of course."

Dufrenne turned to his companion. "Hartmann—the man of the stolen war plans. *Mon Dieu!* Why did I not think of him before?" He seemed deeply chagrined. "Of course—of course—that explains everything."

"Where is Monsieur Duvall to communicate with you?" Dufrenne's companion asked. His voice held a note of brisk authority.

"At the Hotel Metropole. I shall take a room there at once."

"Good. I must leave you for a short time. Await news from me at the hotel. I shall, I hope, be able to inform you, within half an hour, whether our suspicions regarding Dr. Hartmann are correct or not. If they are, you will of course advise Monsieur Duvall accordingly. Above all things, the delivery of the snuff box to Hartmann must be prevented. On that point the Prefect was emphatic." The young man turned into a cross street as he concluded and was swallowed up in the crowd.

Dufrenne, after securing his room at the Hotel Metropole, sat down to wait. He did not have to wait long. The young man, Lablanche, joined him in a short time. "We have just learned," he said, gravely, "that our suspicions are entirely correct. Dr. Hartmann is responsible for the theft of the snuff box, and is momentarily expecting the man who is to deliver it to him."

Dufrenne looked grave. "Duvall should know this without delay," he said.

He had no more than spoken, when the telephone bell in his room rang. He hastened to reply and found Duvall at the other end of the wire. "Come to the Hotel Universelle," the latter said, laconically. "Hurry. I will wait for you."

Dufrenne communicated the message to Lablanche. The latter nodded. "Good!" he said. "Give Monsieur Duvall the information you have, and above all, impress upon him the necessity of acting immediately. There is no time for delay. I will follow at once, with another of our men."

The curio dealer found Duvall pacing anxiously up and down the hotel corridor, pretending to be searching a railway time-table. He nodded imperceptibly toward the cafe as Dufrenne entered, then turned and went out into the street. The old man followed him—in a few moments they were conversing rapidly in the doorway of a near-by shop.

Dufrenne had but a few words to say, but they were sufficient to show Duvall the extreme gravity of the situation. He stood for several moments, considering the best way by which the delivery of the stolen snuff box to Dr. Hartmann might be prevented. Then he signaled a cab which he saw approaching. "Seltz is breakfasting—inside," he said quickly to Dufrenne. "Don't let him out of your sight. I am going to see Dr. Hartmann." He sprang into the cab, gave the doctor's name to the cabman, and in a moment was being driven rapidly up the street, leaving the little old Frenchman standing blinking with astonishment on the sidewalk.

CHAPTER X

When Richard Duvall left the Hotel Universelle, en route to the office of Dr. Hartmann, he had no definite idea of just what he intended to do on reaching there. One thought was uppermost in his mind—he must prevent, in some way, and at any cost, the delivery of the snuff box to Hartmann, and since to follow Seltz to the latter's office would avail him nothing, he decided to precede him there.

During the drive, he began to formulate a plan, daring in its conception, extremely dangerous in its execution, yet one which, if carried out with courage and determination, promised success. He was perfecting in his mind the details of this plan when the carriage turned into the driveway at Dr. Hartmann's.

So occupied had he become with his thoughts that he failed to observe the figure of Grace, standing behind the maid in the open doorway; she disappeared into the reception-room before he had alighted from the cab. He went up to the servant, assumed an air of dignified assurance, and announced that he wished to see Dr. Hartmann at once.

The maid ushered him in, glanced into the parlor, observed Grace sitting there, apparently reading, and then throwing open the door to the left which gave admittance to the doctor's office, bade Duvall enter. The latter stepped in at once, without looking into the room across the hall. Had he done so, he would have observed his wife, whom he fully supposed to be quietly waiting for him in Paris, rise from her chair with a frightened face and start impulsively toward him.

For a moment Grace was on the point of calling out— she wanted to let Richard know that she was there. She wanted to see him—to talk to him, to realize the happiness of being once again in his presence. It had been, since their parting the day before, her constant thought. Then she suddenly realized that Monsieur Lefevre had warned her not to appear to recognize her husband, should she meet him in the course of her adventures. The thought checked her—she paused at the door of the reception-room and glanced down the hall.

The servant who had admitted Duvall had disappeared toward the rear of the house. Everything about her seemed quiet. She started across the hall, determined to enter the room into which Richard had just vanished, when she heard the sound of rapid footsteps approaching her. With a start she turned and again entered the parlor, assuming a careless manner she by no means felt.

She had scarcely seated herself in the chair by the fire, and opened her book, when she saw Dr. Hartmann appear in the hall and enter the door which led to the outer office.

Grace was undecided as to what she should do next. Her safest course, she ultimately concluded, was to do nothing. She remained quietly in her seat, pretending to read her book, but all the while watching, with anxious eyes, the door on the other side of the hall.

Richard Duvall, meanwhile, had entered the waiting room, his mind fully made up as to the course he was about to pursue. During the few moments which intervened, until the doctor's arrival, he looked keenly about the room, examining it in detail, fixing its entrances and exits firmly in his mind, so as to be prepared for any emergency which might arise.

The room was a large one. Along the side facing the entrance door, as well as that which fronted on the park, were big curtained windows, set in deep recesses, and between them, cases of books. At the far end of the room, toward the rear of the house, was another door. Duvall stole over to it, listened carefully, then slowly opened it and looked within. The room proved to be the doctor's private office, and he saw at once that it was built in a sort of ell, and could not be entered except through the room in which he stood. There was a door, it is true, in the right-hand wall, which had once given entrance to the hall, but against this a heavy instrument case, with glass doors, now stood.

Duvall withdrew his head and shoulders from the doorway, nodding to himself in a satisfied way, then noiselessly closed the door and returned to the center of the room.

In a moment Dr. Hartmann came in, glancing at him sharply. "Good-morning, sir," he remarked, in French. "You wish to see me?"

The detective took a card-case from his pocket and tendered the doctor a card. It was one of many which he carried for such emergencies, and bore the name of Stephen Brooks.

"Yes," he said, pleasantly. "I came to consult you concerning a curious case."

"Indeed!" The doctor looked at the card carelessly. "I see that you are an American." He began to speak in English. "Sit down, please."

"Thank you." Duvall took a chair.

"What is the nature of the case, may I ask?"

"Doctor—I've heard so much of your wonderful cures—of your remarkable success in treating mental disorders, that I have ventured to come to you in the hope that you may be able to help me."

The doctor smiled, not displeased at the other's flattery. "What is the cause of your trouble, Mr. Brooks?"

Duvall observed him thoughtfully for a moment. "If a person has delusions upon one particular subject, is he on that account necessarily insane?"

"Not at all. Manias of various sorts are not uncommon, and generally curable. Why do you ask?"

"Because I want you to treat such a case."

The doctor considered his patient narrowly. "Of course, you understand, Mr. Brooks, that my professional charges are very high."

Duvall took out his pocketbook and removing from it a note for a hundred francs, laid it carelessly on the table. "I have understood so, Doctor," he remarked. "Luckily I am a man of considerable wealth."

"In that event," Hartmann remarked, eying the bill in a gratified way, "I am at your service. What is the nature of your complaint?"

"It isn't about myself that I have come," Duvall hastened to inform him. "It concerns a man in my employ—my valet, to be exact."

"Your valet?" The doctor frowned, and made as though to rise. "My dear sir—"

"One moment, please, Doctor. The man is a most worthy fellow. He has been in my service for years. A Belgian, too, I think. I have a very high regard for him— an excellent servant, except for the peculiar delusions with which he has lately become possessed."

"I fear that I cannot undertake his treatment, Mr. Brooks. I receive only a few patients, and those of the highest standing."

"I know that. I did not propose to have the man quartered here in your house. I merely want you to examine him, in order that I may find out whether his case is curable or not. If it is, I shall take him to Paris and place him under treatment—if not, I must, of course, discharge him. It is for that reason that I have come to you."

"What are the man's symptoms?" asked the doctor, shortly.

"He imagines, from time to time, that he has been robbed."

"That is by no means uncommon. I have seen many such cases. Are these delusions confined to any one subject?"

"No. At times he fancies that money has been taken from him. At other times, jewelry that he has never possessed. Once he accused me of robbing him of a pair of shoes, and demanded that I pay him a large sum of money for them. I have generally succeeded in quieting him by assuring him that the stolen articles would be forthcoming later on."

"Excellent. And how long has this condition been in evidence?"

"About a month, now. During the past week, however, the attacks have been more frequent. Last night he informed me that someone had taken from him a diamond ring—of course he had never owned one—and wanted five thousand francs in return. I assured him that I would get him the money this morning."

"The case does not seem particularly difficult, Mr. Brooks, from what you tell me. Of course I could determine better after a personal examination."

"Exactly. And if you find no other conditions of an alarming nature, you think a cure possible?"

"Undoubtedly. When can I see the man?"

Duvall took out his watch. "I requested him to meet me here to-day at noon," he said. "I did not tell him he was coming for a medical examination. He might have refused to come. I let him think that you might be able to recover the diamond ring he thinks has been stolen from him. I thought it best to humor him. I should have brought him with me, but he had arranged to go this morning to see his people, who live in the town. He was to come directly here, after leaving them." He went over to the window and looked toward the road. "I am surprised that he is so late. Usually he is punctuality itself."

The doctor rose. "No doubt he will be here very soon," he remarked. "You can wait here, if you like. I will join you on his arrival. Meanwhile, as I have some matters to attend to in my office, I beg that you will excuse me." He opened the door at the rear of the room, which led to his private office. "When the man arrives, kindly let me know."

Duvall glanced toward the door through which Dr. Hartmann had just passed, then paused for several moments, listening; then he walked noiselessly across the room, and paused before the study door. Within all was quiet. Stooping down, he applied his eye to the keyhole. Dr. Hartmann sat at a large rosewood desk, busily writing.

With a smile of satisfaction the detective arose, and going to the door which led to the hall, drew from the lock the key which stood in it, and then, opening the door slightly, inserted the key in the lock on the other side of the door. As he did so, he peered out across the hall, and for a moment the key almost dropped from his fingers. There, facing him, sat Grace, his wife, whom he had supposed to be safely in Paris. The sight for a moment completely upset him—he paused, gazing at her with an expression of incredulity.

Grace rose, and came toward her husband, her face pale, her lips parted. "Richard," she whispered softly, then became suddenly silent as he pressed his finger to his lips.

As they stood there thus, facing each other in grave uncertainty, Duvall heard the sound of a vehicle being driven up the graveled road. He glanced toward the glass entrance door and saw a cab approaching the house, in which sat Seltz. He turned to Grace, and spoke in a voice so low as to be scarcely audible.

"Open the door at once—before the man can ring. Pretend to be a maid. Show him in here immediately. Quick." He withdrew into the waiting-room, leaving Grace staring at him in amazement. For a moment she hesitated. It seemed so cruel, to be this near to him, and yet to not even be able to touch his hand! Then she went quickly to the front door and threw it open as Seltz came up the steps.

CHAPTER XI

Richard Duvall, alone in Dr. Hartmann's outer office, had not long to wait. He had hardly succeeded in throwing off the agitation which the unexpected sight of Grace had caused him, when the door from the hall was opened, and Grace admitted Seltz to the room.

The latter glanced at Duvall with a curious look, but said nothing. Grace withdrew, closing the door quietly after her. The detective went up to the newcomer and addressed him in a low tone.

"You are Oscar Seltz, from London?" he asked, bluntly.

The man appeared greatly taken back. "Yes," he said, haltingly. "I wish to see Dr. Hartmann."

"About the snuff box, of course?"

Again the man started. "Who are you?" he asked, suddenly suspicious.

"I am Dr. Hartmann's assistant. He has been waiting for you. You have the box with you, of course?"

The man felt carefully in his pocket, and presently drew out a small object done up in paper. "Yes, I have it. The price was to be twenty-five hundred francs."

"That is correct," remarked the detective. "Give it to me."

Seltz drew back his hand. "I want the money first, and I cannot deliver it to any one but Dr. Hartmann."

"Dr. Hartmann is in the next room," said Duvall, with a pleasant smile. "He has the money all ready for you. I will call him. But first, let me see if you have really secured what we want." He held out his hand. "Don't be afraid," he said. "I shall not leave the room. The box will not be out of your sight."

Seltz appeared to consider the matter for a brief moment, but the detective's manner reassured him. He extended the package toward Duvall. "It is there, all right," he laughed, softly. "And a hard time I had getting it."

Without making any comment, Duvall took the package, quickly tore off the coarse paper wrappings, and saw inside a small round ivory box, its top ornamented with a number of small pearls, arranged in a circular design about its circumference. He glanced swiftly at it, crushed the paper into his pocket, then started toward the door at the rear.

"Where are you going?" demanded Seltz, harshly, his hand going toward his pocket, as though for a weapon.

"To call the doctor, my man," Duvall replied. "Don't excite yourself. He will be here in a moment, with your money." Without a moment's hesitation he crossed to the study door and tapped lightly upon it. As he did so, his back was toward Seltz, hence the latter did not see the swift movement, by which he conveyed the snuff box to the pocket of his waistcoat. When, after a few moments' delay, Dr. Hartmann appeared on the threshold, Duvall's hands were both quite empty.

As the doctor entered the room, the detective gave a quick nod toward Seltz. "My man," he remarked, in a low tone. "He seems to be rather bad, this morning;" then aloud, "Oscar, this is Doctor Hartmann."

Seltz bowed, then stood uncomfortably, shifting his weight from one foot to the other as the doctor bent upon him a searching glance. "Sit down, my good fellow," the latter presently remarked, as he took a chair.

"I—I don't think I had better, sir," he stammered. "I am in somewhat of a hurry—"

The doctor interrupted him, in a soothing voice. "There, there. Sit down. I want to talk to you."

Seltz glanced helplessly toward Duvall, apparently somewhat confused by the reception which Dr. Hartmann had accorded him. It was not entirely what he had expected.

"I have explained everything to the doctor," remarked Duvall hastily. "He understands about the money you requested." He looked significantly at Dr. Hartmann.

"Then I hope the matter can be settled at once," said Seltz, apparently much relieved. He made no movement to sit down, but continued to look expectantly at Dr. Hartmann.

The latter nodded in a grave and reassuring way. "Give yourself no uneasiness, my man. Everything will be satisfactorily arranged. Meanwhile, sit down, if you please, and tell me something about yourself. I understand you have been greatly worried, of late. Not quite yourself—let us say."

Seltz looked at him in blank amazement. "I haven't been worried by anything, except the business which brought me here. I want my money—"

"Exactly—exactly," the doctor assented, in a soothing voice. "You shall have your money in due time. I promise you that. But first sit down and let us have a little chat."

Seltz sat down, helplessly. Apparently he was at a loss as to just what to say next. The doctor had told him that the money he expected would be forthcoming—he resigned himself in patience to await the latter's pleasure. For a moment he glanced at Duvall, however. "You should not have taken it from me," he said, peevishly.

Duvall looked quickly at Dr. Hartmann. The latter at once spoke up. "Give the matter no further thought, my man," he said, gravely. "I will see that you are fairly treated. But before we go ahead, I want you to tell me more about yourself—your life—your amusements—"

"What the devil have my amusements got to do with the matter?" exclaimed Seltz, his voice trembling with anger. "I tell you I want my money."

"And I tell you you shall have it. But, now, I insist that you let the matter drop for the present and answer my questions, otherwise I can do nothing to help you."

The remark quieted Seltz somewhat. He was, after all, in a peculiar position. The snuff box was gone. He cursed his stupidity in having let it pass out of his possession before the price agreed upon for its delivery had been forthcoming. That Dr. Hartmann did not question the payment of the money, however, was reassuring. He determined to answer as well as he could whatever questions the doctor might see fit to ask him.

The latter continued to examine his supposed patient with a shrewdly professional air. "How old are you, my man?" he suddenly inquired.

"Thirty-six."

"Do you drink?"

"Yes—I—I drink occasionally."

"Use any drugs?"

"No."

"Appetite good?"

"Yes."

"Sleep well?"

"Yes—pretty well."

"Have you had any shock, recently. Has anything happened to make you nervous, or excitable?"

Seltz glanced nervously from Duvall to the doctor and back again. What, he wondered, was the purpose of this examination? Was Dr. Hartmann trying to lead him into damaging admissions concerning the method he had employed to secure the snuff box? He scowled, then suddenly spoke. "It's none of your affair, is it? if I have."

"Oscar!" said Duvall, in a tone of remonstrance. "Don't speak to the doctor in that way."

"Oscar!" The man turned on the detective angrily. "Look here—you took that—that—" he hesitated, fearful that some trap had been set for him—"that article away from me—now see that I get my money."

The doctor glanced at Duvall. "He seems to be possessed with the one idea," he remarked, *sotto voce*, then turned to Seltz again. "My good man, I have already assured you that Mr. Brooks and myself will see that you get your money. What more do you want?"

"I want the money," Seltz cried, losing his patience, "and I want it quick." He sprang from his chair, and his hand shot toward his pocket, whence it reappeared in a moment with a revolver. "No more of this nonsense, now. I want the cash."

The doctor, who had also sprung to his feet, started toward the angry barber with outstretched hands. Seltz whirled on him, the revolver pointed directly at Hartmann's head. "Keep off," he cried. In his excitement he had forgotten Duvall, who at once seized him from behind. "Look out, Doctor," he cried, as he threw his arm about the fellow's neck and slowly throttled him. "He's gone quite insane—dangerous—take away the revolver."

As he spoke, he tightened his arm about Seltz's throat until the latter gasped for breath. The revolver fell from his nerveless grasp—he clutched at the detective's arm and tried to tear it from his throat, all the while groaning and sputtering at a great rate.

"Hopelessly insane, I fear," said the doctor, as he picked up the fallen revolver. "You had best take him away at once."

"But, Doctor, I can't do anything with him in this violent state. Can't you give him something to quiet him?"

"Nothing but a hypodermic. He wouldn't swallow a drug, I fear."

"Then give him a hypodermic at once. I've got to get him away from here, somehow." He tightened his hold on Seltz's throat as the latter struggled furiously, trying his best to get away. Luckily for Duvall, his adversary was a man of only moderate strength, but he struggled like the madman the doctor supposed him to be, trying in vain to speak. The detective's arm, however, tightly wound about his throat, effectually prevented his cries from becoming intelligible.

"I'm so sorry, Doctor," Duvall went on, as Hartmann prepared his hypodermic needle and approaching the struggling man, took hold of one of his arms and bared it with a quick motion. "I wouldn't have subjected you to all this annoyance for anything. The poor fellow has been getting worse for days, but I had no idea, when he left me this morning, that he would be like this."

"It frequently happens," the doctor remarked, as he pressed the syringe into the man's forearm and then withdrew it quickly. "There—he'll soon be all right now. Just hold him there for a few moments longer, Mr. Brooks and he'll be sleeping like a child."

Even as he spoke, the struggles of the man in Duvall's arms became less violent—his efforts to cry out less vigorous. "It's a sad case," the detective remarked. "I am very much afraid that he must be sent to an asylum."

"Undoubtedly the best place for him, my dear sir," remarked Hartmann, dryly. "I see your cab is waiting, outside. As soon as the man is quiet, I will have one of my attendants help you to carry him to it." He went over to Seltz, who was now struggling faintly, and felt his pulse. "He is quite harmless now," he observed, looking keenly into the man's face. "I will call one of my men." He went to the wall and pressed an electric button.

Duvall allowed the limp body of the barber to slip softly into a chair. "Poor Oscar!" he said, musingly, looking down at the huddled-up figure. "What a pity! Such a faithful fellow, too!" He turned to Hartmann. "I feel almost as though I had lost an old friend."

The doctor smiled. "Rather a dangerous one, I should say," he remarked, as he glanced at the revolver on the table. "You will want this, I suppose."

Duvall took the revolver and thrust it into his pocket. "Might as well take it along, I suppose, doctor. Now about my bill—do I owe you anything in addition to the fee I paid you on my arrival?" He felt for his pocketbook.

"Nothing, my dear sir." The doctor smiled. "I feel that in accepting your fee I am robbing you." He drew the note from his pocket, but Duvall waved it aside.

"I insist, my dear sir. You have given me your valuable time, at least, even if you could do this poor fellow no good." He paused, as an attendant in a gray uniform entered the room.

"Max," said the doctor, addressing the man, "help this gentleman put his friend into the cab."

The man came forward, and he and Duvall picked up the limp figure of Seltz, who was now sleeping soundly. In a few moments they had transferred him to the cab outside.

As they left the house, Duvall saw Grace standing near the door, her face pale, her eyes seeking his. He avoided her glances, making no sign that he recognized her. The doctor, somewhat annoyed, requested her, with elaborate but firm politeness, to withdraw. She did so, without looking back, but her heart was beating until it shook her whole body, and she longed to run to her husband and drive off with him, in spite of the doctor's presence. Somehow she felt that the necessity which had kept her a prisoner in this house no longer existed—that Richard had succeeded in recovering the ivory snuff box, and would soon send her word to join him, so that they might return to Paris together. She went to her room, ordered some luncheon brought to her, and sat down to await his message.

Meanwhile, Duvall, with Seltz beside him, drove rapidly away from the house, his arm about the man's unconscious figure. At the gate of the park he saw another cab waiting, and in a moment perceived that it contained Dufrenne, who in accordance with his instructions had been following Seltz. Duvall nodded to him, then pointed silently down the street. Dufrenne at once ordered his driver to follow. In a short time they had reached the Hotel Metropole, and Seltz, with the assistance of two of the porters, had been carried upstairs and placed on the bed. Duvall explained to the manager of the hotel that the man was a friend of his, who had been taken ill, and needed to sleep for a few hours. He also engaged the adjoining room at once, and thither he and Dufrenne presently repaired to examine the snuff box which, until now, had been reposing safely in the detective's waistcoat pocket.

He drew it out, when they were alone, and silently handed it to Dufrenne. The little old Frenchman took one look at it, then threw up his hands with a cry of joy. "It is the Ambassador's snuff box. Heavens be praised!" he cried, as the tears coursed down his withered cheeks.

CHAPTER XII

Richard Duvall looked at the tense figure, the agitated face of his companion, and once again a feeling of surprise swept over him, as he observed the little Frenchman's joy at the recovery of Monsieur de Grissac's snuff box.

Throughout the exciting events of the morning, and of the night before, the detective had lost sight of the apparent insignificance of the object of their search; now that he for the first time saw it before him, his curiosity was once more aroused. Surely there must be something of vast interest about this apparently worthless bit of ivory, to make its theft the reason for a brutal murder, its recovery a matter of such extreme importance that Monsieur Lefevre should consider the honor of his country at stake.

He took the box from Dufrenne's trembling fingers and examined it carefully. It was about two and a half inches in circumference, and quite shallow, not over half an inch in depth, in all. The ivory was old and yellow from use and time, and very thin and smooth. The lightness of the box surprised him—it seemed to weigh almost nothing, as he balanced it on the palm of his hand.

The circular top of the box was curiously ornamented with a circle of small colorless pearls, of trifling value, set at regular intervals about the edge of the cover. Within this row of pearls was an inscription in Latin, carved in tiny letters in the ivory. From its first words, "*Pater noster*," Duvall saw that it was the Lord's Prayer. The letters extended around the circumference of the box in several concentric lines, or rings, inside of the ring of pearls. In the center of the box was a cross of ivory, carved so as to be slightly raised above its general surface. Beyond this, the box contained no other ornamentation.

Along the front edge of the box Duvall noticed a small spring. He pressed it, in considerable excitement. Evidently the reason for the box's value must be within— some papers, no doubt, of extreme importance. He saw the cover of the box fly upward and glanced hastily inside. The box contained nothing but a few pinches of snuff.

Duvall was almost tempted to laugh. The whole thing seemed so ridiculous—so utterly absurd. Absent-mindedly he tried a pinch of the snuff, inhaling it into his nostrils. It produced nothing more startling than a violent fit of sneezing. Undoubtedly Monsieur de Grissac had told the truth. He did use snuff.

Closing the box, Duvall regarded it for a moment in silence, then looked at Dufrenne. "It isn't worth a hundred francs," he said.

"The box?" answered the curio dealer, as he followed Duvall's glances. "No, monsieur—what you say is indeed true, yet I would not sell it for a hundred million."

"But why? What is there about it that makes it so valuable? Surely you can tell me that, now that we have safely recovered it."

"Alas, monsieur. I could not tell you, even if I knew, which I assure you I do not. I can only say that Monsieur Lefevre has told me that it holds within it the honor of my beloved country, and therefore I would not sell it for all the money in the world."

Duvall was clearly puzzled. "Well," he said at length, as he thrust the box into his pocket, "there's evidently some mystery about the thing that I do not understand, but I suppose I shall, some day. Just at present our first duty is to return the box to Monsieur de Grissac."

"You are right, monsieur, and at once. There is a train for Antwerp in half an hour. From there we can take the night boat to Harwich. Let us set out without further delay."

"And that fellow in there?" remarked the detective with a grim laugh. "We've got to take him with us, you know. He'll be wanted in London for the murder of the man Ncel."

"Yes. That also is important." Dufrenne went into the adjoining room and stood looking at the sleeping barber. "But not so important as the return of the snuff box to Monsieur de Grissac."

Duvall followed him, and lifting one of Seltz's arms, let it drop suddenly. It fell to his side, lifeless. "He's sleeping like a log. The doctor must have given him a pretty stiff dose. I don't see how we are going to travel with him in this condition."

"Then we must leave him in the care of Monsieur Lefevre's other agents here in Brussels. We cannot delay an instant, on any account."

"I do not agree with you, monsieur. There is one thing which is as important to me as the recovery of the snuff box could possibly be to Monsieur de Grissac, and that is, the safety of my wife."

"Your wife?" Dufrenne stared at him in surprise.

"Yes, monsieur, my wife. She is at present in Dr. Hartmann's house. How she came there, I do not know, but I imagine that our friend the Prefect sent her there, to assist, if occasion offered, in our work. In that he was wise; but for her presence, I fear my plan would have failed. Had Seltz rung the doorbell, and been admitted by any of the doctor's servants, I doubt if I should have been able to get the box from him before the latter had seen him. I should then have been obliged to use force, and the results might have been disastrous."

"Yes, monsieur. I see that. The young lady at Dr. Hartmann's was sent by Monsieur Lefevre. His agents here have already informed me of that. But that she is your wife I did not know." He pondered for a moment, glancing at his watch. "It is a great pity. Delay may be most dangerous. Why do you not send her word to join you in Paris?"

Duvall frowned, and began to walk about the room nervously. "A few hours' delay can make no difference," he presently said. "The box is perfectly safe in our hands. I am not, however, at all convinced that my wife is perfectly safe in the hands of Dr. Hartmann."

"But he knows nothing?"

"That I cannot say. So far he does not, I think, suspect that Seltz was the man he expected from London. If he had, he would never have let me leave his office. Luckily for us, Seltz was a stranger to him, and with the murder of Noel on his conscience, he feared to say anything to the doctor about the snuff box while I was present. I imagine he suspected a trap of some sort. But the doctor will discover, probably before the day is out, how he has been tricked. Then he will begin to investigate, and if he finds out that it was my wife who admitted the man, he may in his rage decide to retaliate upon her. I cannot think of leaving Brussels, without her. She must go with me. Upon that I am determined."

Dufrenne looked grave, and a glint of anger came into his eyes. "The service of France, monsieur, is more important than your private affairs. I beg of you that you leave here at once."

"But why, my friend? We can leave just as well in the morning. The box is safe." He felt his waistcoat pocket.

"Safe, monsieur! Let me tell you that neither the box nor you yourself are safe for a moment, as long as you remain in Brussels. You would be in no greater danger, if you were carrying about with you a package of dynamite."

"You are unduly nervous, monsieur," laughed Duvall, as he observed the Frenchman's look of terror. "I have every confidence in my ability to take care of myself. I must notify my wife to join me here as soon as possible."

"How do you propose to do so?" inquired Dufrenne.

For a moment Duvall was puzzled. "You could not safely call her up by telephone," the Frenchman continued. "For her to leave the sanatorium now, in response to such a call, would attract the doctor's suspicion at once. He is probably quite well aware of the fact that she knows no one in Brussels. If he should have her followed here, and see her meet you, he would at once conclude that there was something wrong about the whole affair. He is very well known here in Brussels, and very powerful. Undoubtedly he would have you both arrested on some pretext. Once you are searched, and the snuff box taken from you, all our work is lost."

His earnest face, his frightened tones, disturbed the detective greatly. He saw the force of Dufrenne's arguments, yet the thought of leaving Grace to bear the brunt of Dr. Hartmann's anger was not to be considered for a moment. He looked out of the window in silence for a long time, trying to think out some plan that would insure Grace's safety. A gentle tapping at the door caused him to turn. He nodded to Dufrenne, who at once went to the door and opened it.

The newcomer proved to be Lablanche, of the Prefect's office, whom Dufrenne had met earlier in the day. He bowed to Duvall, who knew him slightly, then glanced at the sleeping figure on the bed. "You have been successful, monsieur?" he inquired eagerly.

Duvall nodded. "This fellow"—he indicated Seltz— "must be taken to London as soon as he is in condition to travel. We will leave the matter to you."

"Excellent, monsieur. He shall be well taken care of. I presume that you and Monsieur Dufrenne will start at once."

"I desire first, Monsieur Lablanche, to get my wife from the house of Dr. Hartmann."

Lablanche gave a low whistle. "I should not advise you to attempt to communicate with her, monsieur."

"You think her sudden departure would make Hartmann suspicious?"

"Undoubtedly."

"Then we must arrange for her to come to Brussels this afternoon on some pretext. If she only had some friends in the city—"

"The American Minister, monsieur!" exclaimed Lablanche, suddenly. "He recommended her to Dr. Hartmann. It appears that he was at one time acquainted with your wife's people. Perhaps he would undertake to telephone to her. That would be entirely safe. But I beg of you, monsieur, do not let the Minister know what your wife's object in going to Dr. Hartmann's was. He knows her only as Miss Ellicott. He vouched for her to Hartmann. If he knew that he had been used, it would make him extremely angry."

For a few moments Duvall stood in silent thought, then picking up his hat, went toward the door. "I will see the American Minister at once," he said, as he went out. "Wait for me here, gentlemen. I will be back within an hour."

Mr. Phelps, the United States Minister, was busy in his cabinet when Duvall was announced. He took the card from his secretary and glanced at it carelessly. The detective's name caused him to start. "Richard Duvall," he said aloud, to his secretary. "Surely it can't be the well-known detective, yet the name—" He regarded the card, his forehead wrinkled with thought. Duvall's distinguished position as the author of several works on the science of criminology was well known to him. "Show him in," he said, at length, and began to relight his cigar.

Duvall was ushered in, and in a few moments had explained the object of his visit. "A young lady—a Miss Ellicott," he told the Minister, "had come to Brussels the night before, and had gone to Dr. Hartmann's as a patient." Mr. Phelps nodded, and added that he had met Miss Ellicott, and had used his influence to enable her to obtain Dr. Hartmann's services. "The doctor is a great friend of mine," the Minister remarked. "I regard him as one of the leading scientists of Europe."

"Undoubtedly," the detective assented gravely. "I am not acquainted with him, myself. My business is with Miss Ellicott."

"Then why have you come here?" asked Mr. Phelps, with some asperity. "The doctor's house is but a few moments' drive."

"I know that. But unfortunately I am not acquainted with Miss Ellicott. She might resent my calling on her so unceremoniously. I had hoped that you might ask her to come here, so that I might be properly introduced to her."

The Minister considered the matter carefully. Evidently he did not altogether like it. "You forget, Mr. Duvall," he said, finally, "that I myself do not know you. Furthermore I certainly have no desire to involve Miss Ellicott in any difficulties. I trust," he concluded, uneasily, "that she is not already so involved."

"No." The detective shook his head. "Not yet. But unless I can have a few words with her in private, she soon may be. I am working in her interests. I am here to protect her from a grave danger." He went toward the Minister, and, taking a package of papers from his pocket, placed them in the latter's hand. "Here are my credentials. From them you will see that I am what I represent myself to be. I cannot undertake to explain to you now the reasons which prevent me from going to Miss Ellicott where she is. The mere fact that I am unknown to her will, I trust, prove sufficient. I wish to say to her but a few words. She will be very glad to hear them, I know."

The Minister returned the papers to Duvall and glanced at the clock upon his desk. "We are having a few friends for dinner to-night, Mr. Duvall. I shall ask Miss Ellicott to join us. If you care to be one of the party—" He paused, looking at the other questioningly.

"I shall be very glad indeed to accept, Mr. Phelps. I assure you that I would under no circumstances force myself upon you in this way, were it not for Miss Ellicott's good. And, in order that your other guests may not by any chance identify me, may I ask that you will introduce me as Mr. Brooks?"

The Minister nodded. "Very well, if you wish it, Mr. Duvall. The whole affair strikes me as extremely unusual, and did I not know you to be a man of your word, I should have nothing to do with it. Under the circumstances, I will consent. At least, I feel sure that no harm can come to Miss Ellicott while she is under my roof."

The detective murmured his thanks. "You will be doing Miss Ellicott a great service, my dear sir," he said. "And one thing more. When you telephone to her, asking her to come, kindly do not mention the fact that I have called." He took the Minister's hand and pressed it warmly. "Some day you will realize the dangers with which Miss Ellicott is being threatened."

On his return to the Hotel Metropole, Duvall found everything as he had left it. Seltz was still sleeping soundly. Lablanche was reading a newspaper. Dufrenne was superintending the placing of Duvall's portmanteau, which had arrived from Paris in response to a hasty wire from him that morning. He had been without a change of linen since the day before, and the arrival of his baggage was gratifying.

He informed Lablanche of his plans. "I shall dine at the United States Minister's," he informed them, "as Mr. Brooks. After dinner I shall ask Miss Ellicott's permission to escort her home. We will take a cab and drive to the railway station in time for the midnight train for Paris. On my arrival there, I shall give the snuff box to Monsieur Lefevre, who will see that it is safely returned to the Ambassador in London. You, Lablanche, can go to London with Seltz as soon as the latter is sufficiently recovered to travel—in the morning, let us say. You, Dufrenne, will no doubt prefer to return with me to Paris. In that event, kindly settle with the hotel people for these rooms, and join me at the railway station." He paused, opened his traveling case, and drew out a suit of evening clothes.

Lablanche and Dufrenne withdrew into the adjoining room, where Seltz lay sleeping. The latter paused in the door as he went out. "Take care of the snuff box," he said, pointedly. "Remember—the honor of France."

CHAPTER XIII

Grace Duvall went to her room, at Dr. Hartmann's, after her husband's departure, her feelings divided between her joy at his success—for she felt that his departure with Seltz meant success—and her sorrow at seeing him leave her, without so much as a single glance. She felt certain that she would hear from him during the course of the afternoon, and after eating her luncheon, sat down to read a book.

The afternoon seemed interminable. When at last she could bear the inaction no longer, she rose, put on her hat, and started down the stairs. As she reached the hall, one of the attendants came up to her. "Someone wishes to speak to you at the telephone, Miss Ellicott," the woman said.

Grace hurried to the 'phone, which was placed in a small recess half-way down the hall. The woman accompanied her, and stood near by as she took up the receiver. Clearly she was listening. Grace determined to speak with caution. It was undoubtedly Richard calling.

When she at last made out that it was the American Minister, Mr. Phelps, who was speaking, she felt a keen sense of disappointment. She learned that he and his wife wished her to come in and dine with them. At first she refused, fearful least by going into Brussels she might miss some word from Richard. Mr. Phelps was insistent. They counted on her. He would not take a denial. The thought occurred to her, momentarily, that possibly Richard had taken this means of communicating with her. The idea seemed far fetched, and yet—she heard Mr. Phelps' voice, urging her to come, and rather half-heartedly she agreed to do so. "The United States Minister, Mr. Phelps, and his wife, have asked me to dine with them to-night," she said to the attendant. "Will you be so good as to have a cab here for me at half-past seven?"

The woman bowed. "Certainly, mademoiselle," she said, and moved aside as Dr. Hartmann came along the hall.

Grace thought that he looked both puzzled and angry. He assumed a pleasant expression as he saw her, however, and when he spoke she knew he had overheard what she had just said. "Dining at the Minister's to-night?" he remarked, as he paused for a moment. "A charming man, Mr. Phelps. I may look in later, myself, and bring you home." He passed on, his face at once resuming the angry scowl which Grace had marked as he approached her.

She returned to her room, and began her toilette for the evening. The small trunk she had brought from Paris contained but a limited wardrobe—she had not expected anything in the way of social engagements, in this work that Monsieur Lefevre had assigned to her. A gown of black satin, however, trimmed with silver, she had put in at the last moment. It was very becoming—Richard had never seen her in it—she hoped he might come to her, before the evening was over. She half-made up her mind to speak to Mr. Phelps about it—to ask him to telephone to the hotels and attempt to locate Richard for her. Then the thought came to her that she had represented herself to the Minister as Miss Ellicott. Clearly it would never do to let Mr. Phelps know that she had deceived him.

She arrived at the house early, and after being introduced to Mrs. Phelps, went to the latter's room to remove her wraps, and to talk over their mutual acquaintances. None of the other guests had as yet arrived. Grace talked to Mrs. Phelps as brightly as she could, but her mind was intent upon Richard, and she wondered when and how she would hear from him.

Duvall, meanwhile, had been engaged in changing his clothes. When he at last put on the white waistcoat of his evening suit, he took up the one he had worn during the day and removed from it the ivory snuff box which had been the cause of his interrupted honeymoon. He glanced at the thing carelessly, before placing it in his waistcoat pocket, and as he did so, he fancied he detected a slight noise in the corridor without. In a moment he had thrown open the door which led to the hall. A man—evidently one of the hotel servants—was just rising from his knees, a small brush in one hand, a dust pan in the other.

Duvall looked at him sharply. The man bowed, smiling in a stupid way, then began to withdraw, explaining that he was cleaning the hall, and hoping that he had not disturbed "monsieur." The detective closed the door, uncertain whether the man had been watching him or not. He remembered Dufrenne's warning, and realized that in going out, alone, this night, he ran some chances of having the snuff box taken from him. Of course, it was unlikely that Dr. Hartmann had any suspicions of him— yet it seemed advisable to put the box in as safe a place as possible, at least until he was once more across the French frontier. Yet where could he put it? To secrete the thing in his room was out of the question. The place might be searched, for all he knew, within half an hour of his leaving it. To conceal it successfully about his person seemed equally impossible. Where, indeed, could he hope to hide an object of this size, so as to defy a search, in case one should be made? His eyes suddenly fell upon the opera hat which he had taken from his portmanteau. He took it up and gazed at it with a smile, then quickly whipped out his knife and began, with great care, to detach the inner lining of the crown for a distance of perhaps three or four inches. Carefully drawing back the lining, he slipped the thin ivory box beneath it, and pushed it back into place. The lining was of heavy black silk, stiffened by the label of the maker which was glued to it. The space between it and the crown was considerable. When Duvall had once more fastened the silk in place with the aid of a needle and thread which he drew from his dressing case, it would have required a very careful inspection, indeed, to have discovered that there was anything unusual about the hat. Even the added weight of the box was not perceptible—its lightness prevented that. When he had completed his task, the detective suddenly threw open the door and glanced into the hall. It was vacant. Evidently he had not been observed.

There were but four guests at the Minister's that night, of whom Duvall and Grace were two. The other two were a Mr. and Mrs. Haddon, friends of Mrs. Phelps, who were making a short stay in the Belgian capital on their way to their home in London.

The little party, with the exception of Duvall, had already assembled in the drawing-room, awaiting his arrival. Grace found the Haddons charming and cultivated people who had traveled all over the world, owing to Mr. Haddon's connection with the English Consular service. Mr. Phelps had told Grace that they were expecting an American, a friend of his, whose name was Brooks, but she did not exhibit much interest in the matter. She was becoming more and more worried about Richard, and wondered if he could, by any possibility, have left Brussels without communicating with her. The thought seemed unbelievable.

Dinner was set for eight. As the hour was striking, the butler announced Mr. Brooks. Grace glanced up carelessly as the latter entered, then her face went white, and she started forward with a glad cry. Mr. Phelps, who was mumbling an introduction, did not, luckily, observe her agitation. Duvall looked at her coolly. "Good-evening, Miss Ellicott," he said, bowing. "I am delighted to meet you."

The shock of the thing almost unnerved her. "Mr. Brooks," she managed to gasp, her face crimson. In a moment she became calmer, as she observed her husband's warning look, and began to chat with him nervously, as though he were the chance acquaintance he pretended to be. In a moment they all were seated about the dinner-table. He had been able to say to her as they left the drawing-room, however, unheard by the others, "I will ask permission to escort you home." She nodded, with a twinkle in her eyes. All her nervousness and anxiety had left her now, and in their place came a delicious feeling of happiness at Richard's presence, and a keen sense of adventure that made the blood tingle through her whole body. "Mr. Brooks!" She laughed inwardly at the thought that no one at the table but themselves knew that they were husband and wife. She proceeded to enter into the spirit of the occasion with huge delight, questioning Mr. Brooks about his business in Brussels with a keen sense of mischief.

It was along toward the middle of dinner that one of the servants came in and handed Mr. Phelps a card. Duvall, engaged for the moment in conversation with Mrs. Haddon, did not perceive it, but Grace, who sat next to their host, experienced a sudden feeling of alarm. She observed the Minister's puzzled face, as he excused himself and left the table, and for an instant she thought of warning Richard. A moment's thought, however, convinced her of the uselessness of the attempt, nor did she indeed know what she could say to him. She remembered Dr. Hartmann's remark, that he might look in at the Minister's after dinner, to which she had attached no importance at the time. Now the thought came to her that the doctor was in the reception-room without, and that his coming, at this time, in the middle of dinner, meant that some disaster was impending.

In a few moments Mr. Phelps reentered the room, followed by Dr. Hartmann. The latter was in evening clothes, and his face seemed peculiarly forbidding and grim.

"Dr. Hartmann has consented to join us," he said to his wife. "Philippe"—he turned to the butler—"lay another place." Then he proceeded to introduce Hartmann to Mr. and Mrs. Haddon and to Duvall.

The latter looked at the doctor calmly. "I think we have met before, Doctor," he said, in an even voice.

"Quite so." Hartmann's face showed not a trace of emotion of any sort. "I hope your servant is better."

"He's still asleep," laughed the detective, then explained to the others, in a few words, his adventure of the morning. He saw that the Minister was puzzled, but the latter said nothing, at the time, and in a few moments the matter was forgotten. Only Grace showed any signs of alarm—Duvall went calmly on with his dinner as though nothing had happened. He spoke to her only occasionally and then addressed her with the formal politeness of a total stranger.

Dr. Hartmann was observing him intently under cover of a spirited conversation with Mrs. Phelps. It was clear to Grace that he could not quite understand why Duvall, or Brooks, as he supposed him to be, was dining here at the Minister's.

It was quite late when the party rose from the table, and, a little while later, Grace, anxious to get away from the place, and be alone with Richard, announced that she must return home. "Mr. Brooks has kindly offered to escort me," she said, quickly, fearful that Dr. Hartmann might suggest that she return with him.

The latter smiled coldly, his eyes fixed on her with a gleam of suspicion. "I think I shall be going myself," he said, as he took leave of the remainder of the party.

As they reached the sidewalk, Duvall observed the taxicab he had ordered to be in readiness, standing in front of the door. He helped Grace inside, then turned in some hesitation to the chauffeur. He dared not tell the fellow to drive to the railway station, since Hartmann, who stood beside the cab chatting with Grace, would inevitably hear him. He therefore instructed the man to go to Dr. Hartmann's with the intention of countermanding the order a little later, as soon as they had got out of earshot of the house. He threw open the door, entered the cab, and was about to pull the door shut after him when he felt his wrist seized from behind in a powerful grasp, and before he realized what had happened, Dr. Hartmann had stepped into the cab and closed the door. The chauffeur at once started off at a great rate.

"I'm sure, Mr. Brooks," said the doctor, suavely, as he sat down in the forward seat, his right hand still grasping Duvall's wrist, "that you will not mind taking me home with you. It is a long walk, and I fear there are no other taxicabs in sight."

Duvall looked at him sternly, then attempted to draw away his hand. "What do you mean, monsieur," he asked, harshly, "by detaining me in this manner?" He again tried to free his wrist, but the doctor was too strong for him.

Hartmann smiled pleasantly. "I feared, Mr. Brooks," he said, "that you might be tempted to use the revolver which you have in the pocket of your coat." He reached over quickly with his other hand and drew the revolver from the detective's pocket.

Grace, through all this, had said absolutely nothing. She realized how fatal any interruption by herself might be. She did not know of her husband's intention to leave Brussels that night. She had heard him order the chauffeur to drive to the sanatorium. Perhaps he wished her to return there. In that event, it was imperative that Dr. Hartmann should not know that the supposed Mr. Brooks and herself were anything but the most chance acquaintances.

"Doctor," she cried out, "what are you doing?"

"It seems that Dr. Hartmann has suddenly lost his senses, Miss Ellicott," exclaimed Duvall angrily.

"Quite so, my friend," said the doctor, sarcastically. "Just as our poor friend Seltz lost his. Don't try anything like that," he snarled, suddenly, as Duvall attempted to release his arm with a sudden twist. "I have a few questions I desire to ask you, Mr. Brooks."

"Questions? What are they?"

"I cannot possibly ask them here, in the presence of Miss Ellicott. Perhaps you will oblige me by stepping into my office for a few moments when we arrive at our destination."

"I can spare you five minutes," said Duvall, sullenly. He could not help remembering Dufrenne's advice, and regretted bitterly that he had not followed it. He had been prepared for almost any contingency. As he left the Minister's house, his hand clutched a revolver in the pocket of his coat. There seemed no way in which Hartmann could prevent him from taking Grace to the railway station. He felt so sure of this that he became overconfident. One moment only had he been off guard— the moment when, with his back to Hartmann, he had stepped into the cab. And the latter, seizing upon that instant's slip, had turned the tables upon him so completely that he cursed himself in his chagrin. Here he was, headed for Dr. Hartmann's house, on the outskirts of the town. Once there, the latter's attendants could easily overpower him and carry him into the place helpless. There seemed no possible means of escape. He determined to brazen the matter out, and meet Hartmann on his own ground. Resistance would at this juncture be useless. He congratulated himself that Grace had, by her cleverness, not shown her hand. The doctor evidently did not suspect, at least not very strongly, that she was anything other than she seemed—a patient. He knew he would be searched, and hoped that the place of concealment of the snuff box would defy even Hartmann. After that, he would demand his release, and rely upon Mr. Phelps to get it for him.

He lifted his head and saw that they were at the house. Without loosening his hold upon Duvall's arm, the doctor called to the chauffeur, "Ring the bell." The latter did so. In a moment, a servant appeared. "Send Max and Rudolph here," cried Hartmann, and presently two husky young Germans came out of the house. Hartmann spoke a few quick words to them in their own language and they ranged themselves on either side of the cab door. Then the doctor threw it open, and released the detective's wrist. "Get out, if you please, Mr. Brooks," he said, with a sardonic smile.

CHAPTER XIV

When Grace arrived at Dr. Hartmann's that night, she was so utterly astonished by the course which events had taken that she was scarcely able to think. What to do she could not even guess. Here was her husband, the man she loved, in the power of Dr. Hartmann, and there seemed nothing whatever that she could do to help him. Yet how could she go quietly to her room, when Richard might be in the gravest danger? On the other hand, to attempt any resistance, to let the doctor know, by any action on her part, that she and Duvall were working in conjunction, would result in nothing but further disaster. The thought flashed through her mind that by preserving her character of a patient, she might, in the morning, communicate with Mr. Phelps, and secure his assistance in obtaining Richard's freedom.

These considerations came and went in the few seconds required for the little party to enter the hall. Her husband went first. Dr. Hartmann stood aside to permit her to follow him. Duvall turned as she passed through the door, and she heard him whisper, in a voice scarcely audible, "Say nothing." It was the cue she desired. She extended her hand as the doctor came in. "Good-night, Mr. Brooks," she said, quite calmly. "Thank you for bringing me home. I hope we shall meet again, sometime."

"I hope so," Duvall remarked, indifferently, then turned to the doctor. "Now, monsieur, let us have done with this farce as quickly as possible. I have no time to waste."

"Nor have I. Good-night, Miss Ellicott." He nodded pleasantly to Grace as she ascended the stairs, then addressed one of the two attendants. "Where is Herr Mayer?" he asked.

"He is waiting for you in the laboratory, Herr Doctor," the man replied.

"Good! This way, if you please." He motioned down the hall. "Be so good, Mr. Brooks, as to proceed at once."

Duvall started off down the hall in no pleasant frame of mind. The whole affair had been bungled by his stupidity. He passed through the door which Hartmann presently opened at the end of the hall, and found himself in a long narrow passage, lit by a single electric lamp. Hartmann closed the door carefully behind him, and came on down the corridor, his footsteps echoing loudly on the concrete floor.

At the end of the corridor a second door confronted them. It was opened by a tall blond man, with a reddish mustache and brilliant blue eyes. "I heard you coming," he said, nodding to Hartmann, then looked keenly at Duvall. "So this is the fellow, eh? Where shall we take him?"

The doctor pointed to an iron door which faced that by which they had entered. Between the two doors ran a narrow corridor, with an iron staircase to the left, leading upward. "In here," he said, shortly, and going to the door, opened it with a key which he drew from his pocket.

Again Duvall cursed his stupidity. For a moment, thoughts of resistance crossed his mind but he at once realized the hopelessness of it, and followed the doctor into the room. The tall man brought up the rear, closing the door silently after him.

The room was pitch dark. In a moment, however, Hartmann had pressed an electric button, and a brilliant light flooded the place. Duvall looked about him curiously, and in that fleeting glance saw that the room was without windows of any kind, and that the walls, smooth and white, contained no openings whatever, except the door by which they had entered. The floor, as he could tell by its feel under his feet, was of cement. The room was bare of furniture, but he perceived a number of boxes and packing cases standing about the walls.

The instant the door was closed, Hartmann sprang at the detective and grasped his two wrists. The latter had always been considered a powerful man, but the arms and shoulders of the doctor were those of a Hercules. "Search him, Mayer," he said, as he pinned Duvall's wrists together in his iron grip.

The man addressed as Mayer at once began a systematic search of Duvall's person. With deft fingers he explored his pockets, felt the linings of his clothing, tore through the contents of his pocketbook. The opera hat had fallen to the floor, in the short struggle which ensued when the detective found himself in Hartmann's grasp. Mayer picked it up, glanced at it carelessly, then threw it angrily into a corner, where it rolled unobserved, into the shadow of a large box.

"There is nothing here," he said, in a voice of keen disappointment. "He must have hidden it elsewhere."

"In his room at the hotel, perhaps—his portmanteau," the doctor said, eagerly, releasing Duvall's hands and throwing him to one side with some violence.

Mayer looked grave. "I have searched everything thoroughly. It is not there."

The doctor muttered an oath. "The other—the old Frenchman?"

"He was arrested to-night on a charge of irregularity in his passport. Nothing discovered. He will be released in the morning."

"*Teufel!*" The doctor swore excitedly in German. "Then the other one—the one who was in charge of Seltz—he must have it."

"No. He also has been searched, with the same results."

"May I ask what you are looking for?" asked Duvall, calmly.

"You know, well enough, Duvall," exclaimed Mayer, turning on him. "Oh, yes—I know your name. The examination of your baggage showed that. As soon as I wired to London and discovered that the man Seltz had left there last night, I knew how we had been fooled. One of our men saw the snuff box in your possession just before you left the hotel to go to the house of Mr. Phelps. What have you done with it?"

Duvall regarded his questioner calmly. "I do not know what you are talking about, gentlemen. I have no snuff box, nor do I use tobacco in that form. And now, if you have concluded this outrage upon an American citizen, perhaps you will let me return quietly to my hotel. If you do not, I promise you you shall pay heavily for it."

His words, for the moment, seemed to disconcert the two men. Then Mayer laughed, "Nothing but bluff, young man—American bluff. I know who you are. You followed Seltz here from London, and got the snuff box from him by a trick. Now tell us where it is."

The detective smiled. "I do not know what you are talking about," he said, quietly.

Dr. Hartmann growled out an oath. "Take off his things, Mayer. He may have the box in his clothing somewhere—or the heel of his boot. I'll get a dressing-gown, from above." He left the room, and Duvall heard him clanking up the iron staircase.

"If you insist on removing my clothes," he said to Mayer, "I prefer to do so myself." He rapidly stripped off his evening suit and shoes, and threw them upon the floor.

The man gathered them up, feeling each article carefully, and testing the heels of the boots with a knife which he drew from his pocket. He appeared greatly disappointed at not finding the object of his search. Then he again examined Duvall, feeling his person from head to toe with great care. He had just finished when the doctor returned with a long gray woolen dressing gown, which he tossed to the detective.

"He's hidden it somewhere. He hasn't got it with him," Mayer exclaimed, angrily.

"Take him to the small bedroom in the west wing," said the doctor. "We'll get it out of him, before we're through. You can leave the clothes in the laboratory." He cast his eye about the room to see that nothing had been forgotten. Duvall trembled, thinking of the hat lying unseen behind the packing case in the corner. Hartmann, however, did not observe it. Without saying anything further he threw open the door, and they all passed into the little hall.

From there, Duvall was led up the iron staircase to the floor above, and found himself in a large room which he took to be the doctor's laboratory. It was dimly lit by means of a reading-lamp. He had a confused vision of a number of scientific appliances, bulking huge and forbidding in the shadows, and then was conducted through a glass door and along a corridor similar to the one through which he and the doctor had so recently passed on the floor below. He judged, from the direction they were taking, that it was directly above the lower passageway, and led back to the main part of the house.

In this he soon found that he was correct. A door at the end of the corridor gave entrance to the upper central hall of the main building. He was led off to the right, catching a momentary glimpse of a woman attendant sitting in a chair near the head of the stairs as he passed. In a few moments Hartmann paused before a door, threw it open, and turned on the lights. The detective saw before him a well-furnished bedroom, with two large windows, and another door, which he later found gave entrance to a bathroom. The dark shadows against the night light without showed him at once that the windows were barred.

He turned to the two men. "You do not intend to release me then?" he asked, angrily.

Hartmann laughed. "You will be quite comfortable here, my friend. I am sure that a few days of complete rest will benefit your condition greatly. I imagine your trouble is merely a temporary affliction—a loss of memory, let us say, an inability to recall your name. We'll soon have you all right again. You have only to inform me where you have placed the snuff box which you stole from my messenger this morning, and I shall know that a complete cure has been effected. If your friends are alarmed about you, it will be quite sufficient to tell them that you are in my care. Mr. Phelps, for instance, has complete confidence in my ability. I will make it a point to explain matters to him at once. Just a trifling ailment, a disordered condition of the brain cells. A week should set you right again. If there is anything you wish, the attendants will get it for you. Your clothes will be sent up from the hotel in the morning. Make yourself quite at home, I beg of you."

He turned away, with a sardonic smile, and Duvall heard the key turn in the door as it closed. He glanced at the barred windows, the door, half-open, leading to the bathroom, and realized that there was not the slightest hope of escape. Dr. Hartmann evidently intended to keep him a prisoner until he disclosed the whereabouts of the snuff box. He smiled grimly as he threw himself upon the bed. It seemed likely that his stay would be a long one.

After a time he began to think of Grace. How cleverly she had carried out her part! It was clear that the doctor did not suspect her, or, if he did, was unable to see where his suspicions led. How strange it seemed to realize that she, his wife, lay somewhere under the same roof with him—possibly even in the very next room! But thirty-six hours had passed since their wedding and their sudden and unexpected parting. During that time, he had seen Grace but twice, once, at Hartmann's office, in the morning; the second time, at the Minister's that night. How he had longed to touch her hand, to put his arms about her, to feel his lips on hers. Yet as matters stood, the chances of their seeing each other in the near future seemed particularly remote. He wondered if Hartmann would keep him a prisoner in his room. The morning, of course, would tell. He switched off the lights, got into bed, and after a long time fell into a broken sleep.

CHAPTER XV

It was late in the afternoon, when Dr. Hartmann, through his man Mayer, discovered that Seltz had left London, and should have appeared at his office with the snuff box during the forenoon. A description of Seltz, together with a curious feeling of uneasiness which he felt after the departure of the man who had introduced himself as Mr. Brooks, caused him to conclude that he had been made the victim of a clever trick, and one which only his professional enthusiasm had made possible.

He at once set to work, through Mayer and his men, to locate Brooks. This was done, without difficulty, at the Hotel Metropole. While the doctor followed the latter to the Minister's, firm in his belief that he carried the snuff box with him, Mayer had arranged through certain connections with the Belgian police, to have Dufrenne arrested and placed in confinement over night on a trumped-up charge; Seltz liberated, and Lablanche held on a pretense of being concerned in the theft from the latter of a valuable package. A thorough search of Duvall's baggage—Dufrenne, it seemed, had none—disclosed nothing, except certain documents setting forth that the latter was Richard Duvall, an American citizen. It was these papers, in fact, which Duvall had shown to Mr. Phelps earlier in the day.

There was nothing to indicate to Hartmann that Duvall was acting in the interests of the French secret police, but the doctor suspected it, knowing as he did that the recovery of Monsieur de Grissac's snuff box would become at once a matter of the utmost moment to Lefevre and his men. Curiously enough, his momentary suspicions of Grace had largely disappeared. There was nothing to connect her with Duvall. He did not know that it was she who had opened the door and admitted Seltz to his house earlier in the day—he thought that Duvall had done this himself. Grace's manner, her conduct during the ride in the cab from the Minister's house, had shown him nothing. Still, he felt that she would bear watching and made his plans accordingly.

The sun was shining through the windows of Duvall's room when he awoke the next morning. For a brief space he was unable to recognize his surroundings, then the sequence of events came to him with a rush. He was conscious of a knocking at the door. He sprang up and opened it. Outside stood one of the men attendants whom he had seen the night before, with the portmanteau containing his clothes. The man placed the bag upon a chair, and opened it, then withdrew.

Duvall proceeded at once to dress. He had just finished when the attendant returned with an elaborate breakfast on a tray. He ate heartily. Evidently the doctor had no intention of starving him. Upon the table he observed his watch and seals, which he had worn with his evening clothes the night before. He looked at the watch and saw, to his astonishment, that it was after nine o'clock.

Now that he was dressed, he wondered what he should do with himself. It did not occur to him that the doctor would do other than keep him confined to his room, yet the man who had brought the breakfast things had not apparently locked the door when he went out.

Without any clear idea of what he intended to do, Duvall went to the door and tried it. To his surprise, he found it unlocked, and in a moment he had passed out into the hall.

The house seemed deserted. Even the attendant who had sat at the head of the stairs the night before was no longer in evidence. He went down to the lower floor without seeing any one. As he passed the door of the doctor's office, on his way to the entrance, he heard it open, and Dr. Hartmann looked out at him with a grim smile. "Ah—going for a stroll, I see, Mr. Duvall," he said, pleasantly enough. "It's a fine morning. I hope you enjoy it."

Duvall made no reply. He appreciated fully that Hartmann was only making fun of him, and realized his helplessness.

Once outside the door, he paused for a moment to drink in the beauty of the morning. Straight ahead of him stretched the driveway which led to the main road. The ornamental iron gate stood invitingly open. He went toward it, unconsciously pondering upon his situation and what he could do, if anything, to escape from it. At the gate he paused, looking about carefully to see whether his movements were observed. There appeared to be no one near him, although along one of the paths to the right of the house, he saw several persons walking, whom he judged to be inmates of the place. One or two others sat on benches among the shrubbery, reading. None of them seemed to take the least interest in his movements.

An empty cab passed slowly, the driver on the lookout for a fare. For a moment the detective thought of escape, his hand came up with a jerk to signal the cabman, then suddenly he let it fall with an exclamation of dismay. He could not escape—he did not dare attempt it, knowing that the snuff box, which had already caused him so much anxiety and trouble, lay in a corner of the room beneath the doctor's laboratory. First he must get that, before he could attempt to escape. He turned slowly back toward the house.

Then suddenly another doubt assailed him. Had not Dr. Hartmann allowed him this liberty merely to see whether or not he would take advantage of it? Would the latter conclude, now that he had failed to do so, that the snuff box was hidden somewhere on the premises? The thought disturbed him greatly.

Still another consideration occurred to him. If he made any attempt to recover the box, would his doing so not show his captors at once that they had overlooked the hat—a chance, indeed, in a thousand? The first move he might make toward the room under the laboratory, would arouse Hartmann's suspicions, a search would be made and the hat and its precious contents discovered.

Certainly he was tied hand and foot. He dared not leave the place, without taking the snuff box with him; he dared not attempt to recover it for fear its hiding place would thereby be disclosed. He was, he suddenly realized, as much a prisoner as though he were locked in a cell. And Grace?

The thought of her caused him to glance about nervously, and in a moment he saw her coming toward him from the direction of the house. She appeared to be looking for him, yet when she saw him, she seemed in doubt as to what to do. Duvall went up to her. "Good-morning, Miss Ellicott," he said, in a voice clearly audible within the house, were any of the windows open. He fancied he detected Hartmann's dark face peering at him from the waiting-room.

"Good-morning, Mr. Brooks," she said, affecting great surprise at seeing him. "You are here still?"

"Oh, yes." His tone was careless, but as he spoke he moved in a direction away from the house, and toward a small bench that stood beside the driveway. "Dr. Hartmann concluded that I needed treatment—I'm afflicted with loss of memory, it seems. Beautiful day, isn't it?"

She murmured some response, waiting for him to speak again. Presently he judged the distance from the house sufficiently great. No one was near enough to possibly overhear them.

"The snuff box is hidden—sewn inside of the false crown of my opera hat," he said, in a low voice. "It is in the room under the doctor's laboratory. He does not know it is there, and I don't dare try to get it, for fear he will find out. If you have a chance—" He paused.

"I understand."

"But be careful—very careful."

"I will." They sat down upon the bench toward which they had been headed. "I had thought of seeing Mr. Phelps to-day, and asking him to have you released."

"It would be useless," he said. "I cannot go without the snuff box."

"Shall I send word to our friends in Brussels?" she asked.

"How can you do that?"

She explained the method, by means of the boy who drove the delivery wagon. He considered the matter carefully. "Let them know that I am here, and why I cannot escape. Tell them that the snuff box is safe—so far. Do not let them know where it is—I trust no one with that—except you, dear."

The tenderness of his voice thrilled her. She longed to grasp his hand—to tell him of the love which filled her heart. Suddenly he spoke, quickly, warningly. "Be careful," he said. "We are being watched. That man Mayer is observing us with an opera glass, from a window of the house. Don't look at me that way. I shall leave you now. Let us meet during the afternoon." He rose, bowed to her carelessly, and strolled back toward the house, leaving her disconsolate upon the bench.

He entered the hall aimlessly, not knowing what to do next. The situation was one which taxed his resources to the utmost. No case that he had encountered in his whole experience offered the slightest suggestion whereby he might hope to effect a solution of his present difficulties. Courage, resource, ingenuity seemed alike useless. He was helpless.

Dr. Hartmann appeared in the hall as he entered it. "Come in, Mr. Duvall," he said, holding open the door of the office. "Suppose we have a little chat."

For a moment the detective hesitated, then decided to meet the doctor's good nature in kind. "By all means," he replied. "You owe me some explanation of your conduct in keeping me here."

"Keeping you here, Mr. Duvall? Surely you are mistaken. The gate is open." He waved his hand toward the lawn.

"I have no desire to run away, like a criminal, Dr. Hartmann. When I go, I shall go in a dignified way, and take my belongings with me."

"Your belongings!" The doctor seemed impressed with the remark. "So you have the snuff box hidden somewhere among them, have you?"

Duvall began a hasty denial, but the doctor cut him short. "Absurd, Mr. Duvall," he exclaimed. "You would leave here quickly enough, if you could take the box with you. But where you have concealed it, I confess I cannot imagine. I have examined your things with the utmost care. It is not among them, of that I am certain. I gave you your liberty this morning, to see whether or not you would attempt to escape. Had you done so I should have known that the box was concealed somewhere in the city, or else in the hands of your confederates. Now I am convinced that it is here. I thought at one time that you might have given it to Miss Ellicott—I have an idea that there is something between you, although of that I am by no means certain. But I know that she hasn't it, for her belongings were searched with equal care, last night, while she slept. The thing is a mystery to me, Mr. Duvall, and I compliment you upon your ingenuity. Had you been as wise, yesterday, as you were clever, you would have left Brussels before I discovered the trick you had played on me. Why you did not do so—why you foolishly remained to dine at the house of Mr. Phelps, I confess I cannot see. It is beyond me. But all that is beside the case. You have the snuff box—at least you know where it is. Are you going to turn it over to me, or must I force you to do so?"

Duvall listened to the doctor with an impassive face. "I know nothing about any snuff box," he returned, with a show of anger. "You are wasting your time, Dr.

Hartmann. I have nothing more to say on the subject." He turned his back and gazed moodily out across the lawn.

Hartmann regarded him with a scowl of anger. "I give you until to-night, Mr. Duvall, to do as I ask. After that, I shall be compelled to force you to do so."

The detective shrugged his shoulders and turned to the door. "You use strong words, my friend. If any harm comes to me, my government will know how to deal with you." His threat did not seem to alarm the doctor particularly. "Do not forget, Mr. Duvall," he said, with an evil smile, "that while I know how to cure mental disorders, I also know how to create them. Good-morning."

The grave threat in his words filled Duvall with uneasiness. What did Hartmann mean? Did he propose to feed him with drugs, cunningly concealed in his food, which would steal away his senses, and leave him a babbling child? The thought was terrifying. Yet he had until to-night. He decided to return to his room and think, hoping thus to evolve some plan which might prove a solution of his difficulties. In the afternoon he would communicate it to Grace, and she, in return, could send word to Dufrenne, so that the latter might cooeperate with him.

He found everything in his room as he had left it, and, seating himself by the window, was soon plunged in deep thought. The arrival of one of the attendants with his luncheon some two hours later woke him from a maze of profitless scheming. The problem was as yet still unsolved.

After luncheon, he decided to go down and have a talk with Grace. By keeping away from the house, and walking through the shrubbery, he hoped to be able to talk with her more freely. Much to his surprise, he found the door of his room once more locked. He sat down with a feeling of utter helplessness. The net was beginning to close about him.

Dinner was brought in at seven, and with it a small bottle of claret. He made an excellent meal, in spite of his unhappy reflections. The claret proved a welcome addition to it. On the tray was also a cigar. Decidedly the doctor was thoughtful, he reflected grimly.

Shortly after dinner he began to feel strangely drowsy. For a time he resisted the feeling—fought against it, but his eyelids seemed weighted with lead. Try as he would, he could not keep his eyes open. He threw up the window, gasping at the fresh air, but it had little effect. He rushed to the door, tried it, found it locked as he had expected, then groped toward the bed and fell heavily upon it, drunk with sleep. "It must have been the wine," he muttered to himself, and in another moment his muscles relaxed and he lay unconscious.

Chapter XVI

When Richard Duvall once more opened his eyes, he saw nothing but a blinding glare of light, that hurt and bewildered him with its singular and brilliant intensity. He closed his eyes again at once, unable to bear the irritation which was thus caused him. It was not exactly pain that he felt, but an intense discomfort, such as one experiences when looking directly at the brilliant rays of the sun.

After a few moments spent in futile attempts to cover his eyes with his hands, only to discover that his arms were tightly bound, he thought to secure relief by turning his face to one side, so that his vision might seek the soft darkness which seemed to lie on every side of him. In this effort he was equally unsuccessful. His head, his neck, his whole body, were rigid, immovable. He could not stir an inch in any direction.

He spent a long time in useless speculation upon the meaning of the remarkable situation in which he now found himself. He felt no pain, no discomfort, except that which the brilliance of the light above him caused. He determined at length once more to open his eyes, in order to discover if possible its source.

Even when his eyes were closed, he could see that the strange light burnt upon them. In a way it rendered his eyelids translucent—he was conscious of a dull pulsing redness through which shot a network of lines of fire. He opened his eyes slowly, cautiously, and looked upward. From some point above him, in what he judged must be the ceiling of the room, extended a beam of violet white light, cutting sharply through the darkness like the rays of a searchlight. At the opening in the ceiling through which it came, this beam was in diameter not more than two inches, but as it extended downward, it widened, taking the form of a long, thin, truncated cone, so that its width, where it impinged upon his face, was perhaps equal to twice that of a man's hand.

The darkness of the room about him made the beam of light seem a tangible, material thing. Its brilliance was unwavering—it extended from the ceiling to the surface of his face with the solidity, almost, of some huge, glittering icicle. He felt as though, were his hands but free, he could brush it aside, fling it off bodily into the darkness.

The effort of looking directly at the source of the light made his eyes smart with pain, but he found that by half-closing them, he could look off into the darkness, through the brilliant cone. In the pathway of its rays danced and tumbled innumerable dust specks—he knew then but for their presence, to afford the light a reflecting surface, its rays would be invisible to him.

In color the light was not yellow, like sunlight, but had a cold violet-blue quality, more nearly resembling moonlight. Its intensity, as well as the shape of the light cone, made him conclude that it was being focused through a powerful lens, or projected by means of a brilliant reflector.

He could imagine no possible reason for the situation in which he found himself. What the purpose of the beam of light was; why it thus focused upon his upturned face, he could not guess. He thought about it for many minutes, his eyes closed, his head straining restlessly toward the soft outer darkness. Presently there flashed into his mind Dr. Hartmann's words at their last meeting: "While I know how to cure mental disorders, I also know how to create them." The thought made him shudder. Was this, then, the explanation of his predicament? Somewhere he had read, not long before, a newspaper account of the investigations of certain Italian scientists, concerning the effect of the violet and ultra-violet light rays upon the cells of the brain. He could not recollect just what the conclusions had been, but he did remember that the newspaper article spoke of the popular superstition that moonlight could cause insanity. He knew Hartmann to be a scientist of vast ability and resource, and realized that back of the elaborate preparations he had evidently made must lie some sinister purpose.

For what seemed an eternity he lay thinking, unable to come to any rational conclusion. The distressing effect of the light rays increased, rather than diminished, as his nerves became more and more unstrung. It seemed, even with, his eyes closed, that he could feel the *weight* of the cone of light upon his face. The desire to escape from its searching glare became well-nigh irresistible. How long would this torture continue? He began to feel intensely tired and worn out and realized that could he but shut out the blinding brilliancy which enveloped him, he would sink exhausted to sleep. Sleep! He could no more sleep, under the present conditions, than he could fly to the moon. Then there came to his mind a recollection of a form of torture practised among the Chinese, the prevention of sleep. Prisoners, he had read, were confined in a cage, in brilliant sunlight, and prevented from sleeping by being prodded from without with spears. At the expiration of a week, he had read, the victim goes raving mad. Was this, then, Hartmann's intention?

Whatever the man did, he knew he would adopt only such methods as would involve him in no damaging consequences. He might be kept in his present situation until insanity ensued, and Hartmann with his reputation as a physician, a scientist, could calmly deny any story he might tell, putting it down to the wanderings of a disordered brain. He realized the cunning of the man, his care to use no physical violence. Should he, Duvall, under the strain of the torture which he realized lay before him, consent to disclose the whereabouts of the ivory snuff box, in return for his liberty, what could he do, in retaliation? Hartmann would calmly deny his story, and would doubtless produce witnesses, such as Mayer, to prove that the detective came to him for treatment for some slight mental disorder, some lapse of memory and that the exposure to the light rays had been but part of his usual treatment. Clearly the doctor had covered his tracks most successfully.

Throughout all these torturing thoughts, the figure of Grace came and went unceasingly. What would she do—what could she do, to aid him? He had warned her not to ask Mr. Phelps to take any steps looking to his release. He realized that were Hartmann to appear now, and give him his freedom, he would not dare to accept it. That the doctor might do this very thing was his greatest fear. If he should insist upon his leaving the place, what could he do, then, to recover Monsieur de Grissac's snuff box? He prayed fervently that Dufrenne and his companions might in some way work out a plan to set matters right.

Presently he fell to thinking of the snuff box, and its safety. How fortunate it seemed, that the doctor and his man Mayer had overlooked the opera hat. He wondered if they had thought of it since? It was clear that they had not, else he would no longer be kept a prisoner. What was the room beneath the laboratory used for? Its appearance had suggested that it was not used at all—a mere lumber-room, a place for storing boxes and crates. And then there flashed into his mind the thought, where was he now? From the apparent distance of the ceiling, as shown by the beam of light, he concluded that he was lying on the floor, a conclusion which the hardness and coldness of the surface beneath him amply proved. Evidently it was a floor of stone, or cement, not one of wood. A certain sense of familiarity in his surroundings came over him. The faint radiance which was diffused about him by the light cone showed the walls before and on either side of him to be of uniform blackness, unrelieved by any suggestion of windows. He strove with all his power to pierce the shadowy gloom, to come upon some point of recognition, but the darkness baffled him.

In one corner a huge shadow, bulking formless against the wall, suggested the packing case behind which his opera hat had been tossed by Mayer during the search the night before. The thought thrilled him with renewed hope. What more likely place, after all, for Hartmann's deviltries than this silent room beneath the laboratory? If he was lying there now, and chance of escape should come, he might even yet be able to take the missing snuff box with him.

The hours dragged interminably. He was conscious of a keen feeling of pain, a smarting irritation, in his eyes, which caused tiny streams of moisture to trickle beneath their lids and roll unheeded down his cheeks. The muscles of his neck became sore and swollen, from his incessant though useless effort to turn aside his head. A dull pain began to shoot insistently through his temples, and his limbs became numb and cold. The desire to escape from the relentless brilliance of the light cone became unbearable; he felt as though, if relief did not soon come, he would shriek out in a madness of terror. Then the hopelessness of doing so became apparent, and he nerved himself with all the power of his will to endure the ever-increasing torture. Yet this torture was, he knew, largely mental—the actual pain was by no means unbearable; it was only the dull, insistent pounding of the light rays upon his eyes, his brain, from which he longed to escape. With closed eyes and tensely drawn nerves, he waited, watching the endless play of the tracery of light in the dull redness of his eyelids.

The sudden sharp rattle of a key in the door, followed by the turning of the knob, told him that someone was entering the room. He had a momentary vision of a patch of light, yellow against the surrounding blackness, which disappeared almost instantly as the door was closed. Then he was conscious of a shadowy form beside him, and heard the smooth, modulated tones of Dr. Hartmann's voice.

"Well, Mr. Duvall," he said, "how goes the treatment? Memory any better this morning?"

He made no reply. The mockery in the doctor's voice roused him to sudden and bitter anger.

"I'm trying a new modification of the light treatment upon you," Hartmann went on, with a jarring laugh. "Dr. Mentone, of Milan, has great hopes of it. Wonderful thing, these violet rays! Have you read of their use in sterilizing milk? No? The subject would interest you. How is your mind this morning? Somewhat irritated, no doubt. Well, well, that will soon wear off. You've only been under the treatment six hours. Scarcely long enough to produce much effect. We'll make it ten, the next time. It is necessary to increase gradually, in order not to superinduce insanity." He went to a switch on the wall and pressed it, and instantly the cone of light disappeared. Another movement, and the room was flooded with the yellow glow of an electric lamp, which seemed dingy and wan, compared with the cold brilliance which it displaced.

The dispelling of darkness brought to Duvall's brain a rush of sensations, among which the knowledge that he was once more in the lumber-room beneath the laboratory stood forth with overwhelming prominence. He glanced at Hartmann with reddened eyes. "Let me up, damn you!" he shouted.

The doctor bent over him, his face smiling. "Just a moment, Mr. Duvall. Have a little patience." He began to unbuckle several straps, and presently stood back, with a wave of his hand. "Get up," he said.

The detective's swollen muscles, his stiffened limbs, still retained the sensation of being bound; he scarcely realized that his bonds had been removed. Painfully he crawled to his feet, and stood before the doctor, blinking, trying to collect his faculties. On the floor lay a number of broad leather straps, secured to iron rings which had been let into the cement floor.

His first thought was to make a quick rush at his captor, and after overpowering him, secure the snuff box and dash from the place. His eyes must have shown something of his intention, for Hartmann, stepping back a pace, drew his right hand from his pocket. It contained an ugly-looking magazine pistol. "Don't attempt anything rash, Mr. Duvall. It would be useless. Even should you succeed in disposing of me, which I hardly think possible, you could not get away from my man Mayer, who is waiting in the corridor outside. Enough of this nonsense," he went on, scowling. "I mean to be quite frank with you, my friend. I intend to subject you to this device of mine—" he waved his hand toward the opening in the ceiling— "until you disclose the whereabouts of the snuff box. I know it is somewhere near at hand, either here or in Brussels, for your two assistants, whom I have had released, have been hanging about the place all the morning. If the violet rays have no other effect, they will at least prevent you from sleeping, and my experience shows that loss of sleep, if persisted in, will shatter the best set of nerves on earth. You know what the effect is, for six hours. The next time, as I said some little while ago, we shall try ten—and after that, longer periods, until the process becomes continuous. I am giving you these brief respites, at first, because I have not the least wish to drive you mad—all I ask is the snuff box which you took from my messenger Seltz. Give it up, and you can go at your convenience. But I must have it—even if I am obliged to drive you to the limit. I advise you to save yourself much suffering, and give it to me now."

The detective drew back his arm—his fist clenched. The impulse to drive it into Hartmann's face was overpowering. He turned abruptly on his heel, and made no reply.

Hartmann waited for a moment, then seeing that his prisoner was not disposed to answer, went toward the door. "Max," he called, opening it, "bring in the tray." The attendant at once entered with a waiter containing food, which he placed on a box near the door. "Is that all?" he asked. Hartmann nodded and the man withdrew.

"Think the matter over, Mr. Duvall," the doctor remarked, as he stepped across the threshold of the door. "I shall call upon you again, later in the day."

Duvall waited until the door had been closed and locked, and the doctor's footsteps had died away up the iron staircase. He heard them for a moment, on the floor of the room above, then all was quiet.

In a moment the detective had stepped to the large box in the corner, behind which lay, he believed, the discarded opera hat. At a glance, he saw that it was still there. He was about to stoop and pick it up, when a sudden fear swept over him. Suppose he was being watched. The doctor was in the room above. The presence in the room of the beam of light showed clearly that there must be an opening in the ceiling, into the laboratory. For all he knew, Hartmann might be observing his every movement. He stopped in his attempt to pick up the hat, and pretended to be greatly interested in the box and its contents. After making a careful examination of the labels upon it, he strolled carelessly back to the other side of the room, and ate the breakfast which the attendant had left. He supposed it to be breakfast, although he had no realization of the time. In a moment he felt for his watch, and found that it was still in his pocket. When he consulted it, however, he saw at once that it had run down.

After his meal, he began to feel terribly tired and sleepy. At first he fought off the feeling, realizing that his only hope of freedom lay in keeping awake, with all his senses alert. Then he thought of the nerve-racking hours through which he had just passed; the many more which were likely to follow, and decided that he must have rest at any cost. He threw himself upon the floor, his head pillowed upon his arm, and was soon sleeping the deep sleep which follows utter exhaustion.

CHAPTER XVII

All during the afternoon of the day upon which she had first met her husband during his confinement at Dr. Hartmann's, Grace Duvall wandered about the place, looking for him, waiting with growing fears for his appearance. When evening came, and she had failed to find him, she became greatly alarmed. In her excitement, she forgot the word she had agreed to send into Brussels by the boy who drove the delivery wagon, and was just returning to the house when she heard someone calling to her from the drive. She turned and saw that it was the bread boy, who had stopped his cart some little distance from the veranda.

"Mademoiselle," he called, "you have dropped your handkerchief." He pointed with his whip to a white object which lay in the roadway close beside the wheels of the cart. She had not dropped her handkerchief—she knew that it was at that moment tightly clenched in her left hand, but she understood.

"Thank you," she called, and hurried toward him. The boy, meanwhile, had climbed down from the wagon, and picking up the handkerchief, which he had himself secretly dropped, handed it to her, with a polite bow. She felt, as she clutched the bit of linen, that within it lay a note.

"He is here," she said quickly, in an undertone. "The box is safe. It is hidden. They have not yet discovered it. But I am afraid something terrible has happened to Mr. Duvall. Tell them to send help, quick." She turned away, and the boy mounted his box, whistling gayly, and at once drove off.

Grace hurried to her room, to examine the note within the handkerchief. She could hardly wait to see what it contained. The contents were a great disappointment to her. "Leave the house about ten o'clock to-morrow morning," it said. That was all. She had already decided to do this, in order to effect, if possible, her husband's release. So far as the snuff box was concerned, she felt that she did not care whether the doctor discovered it or not, if only she might know that Richard was safe. All during the evening she wandered aimlessly about the house, hoping each minute that she might come upon him, but her search was in vain. Richard Duvall seemed to have vanished completely.

Once she met the doctor, just as she had given up in despair and was returning to her room. He spoke pleasantly enough, asked her how she felt, and showed much concern that she had refused to eat any supper. "You must eat, mademoiselle," he told her. "Have you taken regularly the tonic I prescribed?" She nodded, not considering it necessary to inform him that she had carefully poured it, dose by dose, into the sink. For a moment she thought of asking him what had become of Mr. Brooks, but she feared to rouse his suspicions. "I'm feeling somewhat out of sorts," she said. "I'll be all right in the morning."

"I am gratified to observe," he remarked, as she left him, "that you had no tendency to walk in your sleep last night. I trust the improvement will continue. Good-night." She could not determine whether or not there lay any hidden meaning back of his words. His mirthless smile somehow made her feel uncomfortable.

His words, however, inspired her to form a new plan. She would go to the laboratory that night, if she could by any means escape the vigilance of the woman on guard in the hall, and find out, if possible, whether or not Richard was confined there. From the windows of her room, which faced the rear of the house, she could see plainly the small square brick building in which the laboratory was located. There were lights in the floor on a level with her windows—that, she knew, was the room in which she had seen Hartmann sitting at his desk, on the night of her arrival. But there were, she knew, rooms both above and below this one, and in the latter lay hidden the Ambassador's snuff box. Was Richard confined there, as well? She determined to find out.

The woman who sat on watch in the hall came to her room at half-past ten and looked in to see if she required anything. Grace, who was just getting into bed, told her that she did not, said good-night sleepily, and asked her to turn off the lights. The woman did so, and closing the door softly, retired.

Grace lay in bed a long time, wondering how she could get down the hall, and into the passageway leading to the laboratory, without being observed. There seemed no possible way of accomplishing this, yet she was determined to attempt it. Her thoughts were interrupted by the faint ringing of an electric bell. She knew it was the one in the hall, near where the nurse sat, by which any of the patients, desiring her presence during the night, might summon her to their rooms. Grace slipped out of bed, opened her door the slightest crack, so that she could command a view of the hall, and peered out. She saw the nurse coming toward her with a glass of water in her hand. She disappeared for a moment into a room across the corridor, then reappeared almost at once and resumed her seat at the head of the stairs.

Grace was disappointed. She had been on the point of starting out, when the woman's reappearance prevented her. She crouched on the floor beside her door, waiting until the nurse should again be summoned away.

She waited for hours. She heard the church bells in the city, far off and muffled, booming the hour of midnight. The nurse on the chair yawned and nodded. After what seemed an eternity, she heard one o'clock strike, and then two. The house was shrouded in silence. Her knees were cramped and cold, from contact with the floor; her whole body seemed sore, from the nervous tension of her position. She almost screamed, when the electric bell suddenly rang out again, its sound intensified by the stillness until it seemed as though it must wake everyone in the house.

The nurse rose sleepily, glanced at the indicator on the wall which informed her from which room the summons had come, and started down the corridor toward the west wing of the building. As she passed beyond the circle of light cast by the electric globe in the central hall, Grace pushed her door open and slipped noiselessly out. For a moment she hesitated, saw the woman enter a room midway of the corridor, then flew like the wind toward the door which gave entrance to the passageway leading to the laboratory. Her bare feet made no sound, she gained the door without being discovered, and in an instant had swung it open, and was standing in the long covered way outside. She drew the door to after her noiselessly, then sank upon her knees and listened. In a short while she heard the nurse come shuffling down the corridor, and the creaking of her chair as she sank heavily into it. So far, she felt that she was safe.

She advanced along the corridor with great caution. Her chief fear was that the door of the laboratory might be locked, in which case, she would be unable to proceed further. When she reached it, and felt it yield as she slowly turned the knob, she heaved a sigh of relief. In a moment she was in the laboratory.

The room was unlighted, save for a faint glow which came from a small black box in the center of the floor. She had no idea what this box was, but noticed that heavy wires ran to it, from each side, and that there were several protuberances upon its top, which shone like brass. She did not stop to examine it further, however, but looked about for some means of reaching the room below. The idea of recovering the snuff box had suddenly occurred to her. With that in her possession, Richard, she believed, need no longer hesitate to escape at the first opportunity. He had told her that it was hidden in the room beneath. She ran quickly down the steps which she observed in one corner, feeling a glow of excitement at the daring of her quest.

At the bottom of the stairs she found a narrow little corridor with a heavy door opening on it which she judged led into the room she desired to enter. The corridor was lighted by a single window at the end opposite the staircase, through which came a faint light from without.

She groped about in the semi-darkness until she found the knob of the door and slowly turned it, pressing her weight against the panels. It did not yield. With a sickening feeling of disappointment she realized that it was locked.

She stood still for a moment, wondering what she should do next. Suddenly she shuddered, and a horrible faintness came over her. From within the room she distinctly heard the slow moaning of someone evidently in great pain. Thoughts of Richard at once rushed through her mind; she flung herself on her knees, in an agony of fear, and sought frantically for the keyhole. At last she found it, and looked into the room. The sight that met her gaze sent her reeling backward. There lay Richard, her husband, upon the floor, his face encircled by a ring of blinding light, by which she could see, with frightful distinctness, the ghastly expression of his features, the lines of agony about his eyes and mouth.

For a moment she beat frantically upon the door, calling to him incoherently. She thought he did not hear her, for he did not turn his head. Then she stopped, frightened at what she had done. Suppose the doctor were to overhear her? Everything would be lost. There was but one chance for Richard now, she felt, and that lay with her. She would leave the house, in the morning, proceed at once to the Minister's, and tell him the whole story. Snuff box or no snuff box, she was determined to rescue her husband from his present situation, if it was not already too late.

For a long time she looked into the room, watching the face, grim and silent in the circle of light. She called to him over and over, softly, telling him of her plans, of her love for him, of her sorrow, but he seemed not to hear. But for the twitching of his face, and the low moans which he uttered from time to time, she might have supposed him dead.

How she got back to her room, she could scarcely have told. She staggered up the stairs into the laboratory, out along the corridor, and at last reached the door leading into the main building. She pushed this silently open, and gazed cautiously into the hall. The nurse sat in her chair, apparently asleep. With the utmost care, Grace managed to enter the hall, and to close the door behind her. Then seeing that the woman was rousing, she determined upon a bold plan. She opened her eyes wide, trying to give them a vacant, staring appearance, and with arms extended started toward the nurse.

The latter rose with an exclamation of alarm, then recognizing the sudden apparition as Grace, came up to her, took her by the arm, and led her back to her room. She sank helplessly upon the bed, and pretended to fall asleep. Whether the woman suspected her or not, she could not tell—she noticed that she locked the door, on leaving the room.

The hours until dawn seemed interminable. She lay in bed, praying that there might yet be time in which to save Richard from Hartmann's machinations. What it was that the latter was doing to him, she could not guess, but the look of agony on Duvall's face told her that his sufferings, from some cause, were very great.

After a long time the day broke, and she dressed and managed to choke down a little breakfast. She kept in her room until long after nine o'clock, not daring to leave the house before ten. Dr. Hartmann came in just as she was preparing to go. She saw him glance quickly toward her hat, as she put it on. "I'm going in to the city, this morning, doctor," she said, carelessly. "There are a few things I must get at one of the shops."

He nodded, as though the matter were quite unimportant. "You had another attack, last night, Miss Ellicott," he said. "I regret that the symptoms have recurred."

"Did I? What did I do?" she inquired, wide-eyed.

"Nothing, luckily. Walked down the corridor a short distance, the nurse tells me. She stopped you before you got very far." He regarded her with his keen professional look. "Strange—you do not appear abnormally nervous. I fear I shall have to begin the hypnotic treatment at once."

She paid but scant attention. If she could accomplish what she hoped, this morning, neither Dr. Hartmann nor his treatments would matter in the least to her. "I am sorry it will be necessary," she said, "but of course you know best."

When she left the grounds, she watched carefully to see if she was being followed, but there was nothing to indicate that such was the case. At the corner below, a small, youngish-looking man turned in behind her. He appeared to have been walking rapidly, but she had no particular reason to believe that he was following her.

She made at once for the center of the town, determined to walk the distance rather than wait to find a cab. On the way she passed several stores, and it occurred to her to stop in at one of them and buy a pair of gloves, to lend color to her excuses. She did so, and was just going out again when she suddenly came face to face with the young man she had thought was following her. "Miss Ellicott," he said, raising his hat, and as his hand was poised before her eyes, she saw on his finger a ring similar to the one which had been given her in Paris by Monsieur Lefevre, on the day of her departure. She colored, started to pass on, then stopped. "Good-morning," she gasped, faintly.

"I'm so glad to see you," he rattled on. "Don't you remember our being introduced, at dinner one night, in Paris. I'm delighted to meet you again. On your way down-town, I suppose?" His remark seemed a question.

She answered it at once. "Yes, a little shopping to do, and then I thought of stopping at the house of some friends— the United States Minister," she added, by way of explanation.

The stranger bowed. "May I have the pleasure of accompanying you?" he asked. "I also am going in that direction."

Grace assented, and they went out together. At the door the man summoned a cab. "It is safer," he whispered. "We may be observed."

Once inside the cab, which was a closed one, the young man began to ply Grace with questions. "I am one of Monsieur Lefevre's men," he told her, noting her momentary hesitation. "Be quite frank, please, and tell me everything."

When she had finished her story, he sat in silence for a long time. Then he turned to her with a question which made her think he had suddenly lost his mind. "Has Dr. Hartmann a phonograph in the house?" he inquired.

"A phonograph?" she looked at him curiously.

"Yes—yes." His voice betrayed his excitement. "We must send a message to Mr. Duvall. Your windows overlook the room where he is confined. He may hear it. It is the only way."

"Yes," she said, after a moment's thought. "There is a phonograph in the library—a small one. It is seldom used. But Dr. Hartmann—"

"Listen to me," he interrupted, "and do exactly as I say. Pretend to be ill. Ask Dr. Hartmann's permission to have the instrument moved to your room. Then play the records which I am about to get for you."

She gazed at him, scarcely understanding. "But—" she began.

"Of course you will play other records, as well, but this one you must play often—as often as possible. I do not know that Mr. Duvall will understand what the message is—it is a chance, but we must take it. I myself do not understand it very clearly, but the suggestion comes from Monsieur Lefevre himself. You know him. He has your husband's safety at heart." He leaned out, giving a few rapid instructions to the cabman, and then once more turned to Grace.

"Do not visit the house of the United States Minister. It will be most unwise. As soon as he learns that Mr. Duvall and yourself are at Dr. Hartmann's house as spies, he will of necessity refuse to assist you further. Should he not do so, should he demand Mr. Duvall's release, nothing would be gained, since the snuff box would of necessity be left behind. Dr. Hartmann will not injure your husband—he is too anxious to get possession of the snuff box for that. We will try the phonograph, to-day, and if that means is unsuccessful, we must make an attempt to regain the box, and release your husband by force."

As he finished speaking, the cab drew up at a music store. The stranger sprang out, and in a few moments reappeared with a small package in his hand. He handed it to her, then removed his hat and bowed. "I would suggest, mademoiselle, that you return at once, and make use of this as I have directed. If anything further occurs, send word by the delivery boy to-night." He bowed, and walked rapidly down the street.

Grace sadly ordered the cabman to return to Dr. Hartmann's, and then sat back, her mind torn by conflicting emotions. The whole thing seemed inexplicably mysterious and confusing. Here was Richard, her husband, suffering she knew not what agonies at Dr. Hartmann's hands, and these people, who ought to be attempting to liberate him, asked her to play upon the phonograph. She tore open the package which the young man had handed her, and glanced at it eagerly. Its title told her no more than the stranger himself had done. She read it over and over, aimlessly. It was *The Rosary*.

CHAPTER XVIII

The dull, heavy sleep into which Richard Duvall had fallen, after Dr. Hartmann had left him, was suddenly disturbed by the realization that someone had seized him roughly by the arms. He attempted to rise, struggling instinctively against the two men who, he dimly saw, were bending over him, but his resistance was useless. In a moment the leather straps which encircled his wrists and ankles had been drawn tight, and he felt himself being lifted bodily and deposited on the floor in the center of the room. At first he cried out, cursing his captors loudly, but an instant's reflection showed him how profitless his remonstrances were, and he allowed himself to be bound to the floor in silence. In a moment, Dr. Hartmann—the detective saw that it was he, with Mayer—had switched on the violet light, and he once more felt its blinding radiance upon his face.

Hartmann opened the door. "I shall be back again in a few hours," he said, as he left the room. "I hope that by that time you will have quite recovered your senses."

The detective made no reply. He had definitely made up his mind upon one point: he was not going to purchase his freedom at the expense of his duty. The unfortunate situation in which he now found himself was, he knew very well, entirely his own fault, and his desire to atone for his momentary carelessness made him determined not to accede to Dr. Hartmann's demands. He hoped that his friends outside—Lablanche, Dufrenne, even Grace— might be able to come to his assistance. If he could only know that the snuff box was safe in Monsieur Lefevre's hands, the rest did not matter much.

These thoughts passed through his mind as he lay with closed eyes, his face quivering under the dazzling light which fell upon it. Its intensity was, he thought, greater, if anything, than it had been before, and the irritating effect upon his eyes more pronounced. He did not open his eyes at all, on this occasion, for fear even a momentary exposure would increase their sensitiveness.

Slowly the day passed. He concluded that it was afternoon, when he heard far off a bell striking the hour of two, although it might equally well have been two o'clock in the morning, for all he could tell. There was a faint hum of conversation in the laboratory above him, which convinced him that it was still day.

Presently his ear, acutely sensitive to the slightest noise which might disturb the stillness about him, became aware of a faint sound of music, which seemed to come to him from a long distance off. It was a popular French march, and from a certain quality of the notes he concluded that it was being played upon a phonograph. The strains of the music distracted him, took his mind from the things about him, and as he listened to it, it seemed that the effort of keeping his eyes tightly closed grew sensibly less, the blinding pressure of the unwavering light cone upon his face appreciably easier to bear. He knew that this was but a momentary relief, but he welcomed it eagerly. Lying in this terrifying silence, under the cruel glare of light, had become frightful—he wondered if, after all, his nerves, his mind, could long stand the strain.

The music stopped suddenly. He found himself eagerly hoping that there would be more. In a few moments it began again, and he was listening to the familiar strains of *The Rosary*. He had always liked the song—Grace, too, had been fond of it. He wondered if she could be playing to him, trying to soothe his fast-shattering nerves with music. It pleased him to think that it might be so, although he had no reason to suppose that Grace knew of the torture to which Dr. Hartmann was subjecting him.

After a time, the final strains of *The Rosary* died away, to be followed by a German march, played by some military band. This, too, he was glad to hear, although he found himself thinking that he preferred *The Rosary*. As if in answer to his thoughts, it began again—he found himself repeating the words to himself mechanically, and thinking of Grace.

The music continued for long over an hour. Duvall noted with surprise that while there were many other selections, *The Rosary* was played almost every other time. So often, in fact, did its strains break the stillness, that he became annoyed—in his nervous state this constant repetition of the song worried him. After a time he shuddered when he heard it, hoping that each time would be the last. No one but an imbecile, he muttered to himself, could enjoy playing a piece over and over in that aimless fashion. When at last the impromptu concert had ceased, and the silence about him was once more unbroken, he found himself puzzling in vain over the matter, as though it had become of vast importance to him.

After the music ceased, he realized how much it had helped him to endure the two or more hours which had elapsed since Hartmann left him. His real tortures were only just beginning. The constant blaze of light on his face, the ceaseless effort to keep his eyes closed, to turn his head away, in spite of the bonds which prevented it, once more almost frenzied him. He fell to wondering whether Hartmann had been in earnest, when he told him of the qualities of the violet rays. Could they in any way affect his mind? The mere thought stimulated his imagination to such an extent that already he was convinced that his senses were wandering—that his mind was becoming sluggish and dull.

As hour after hour passed, this thought became almost a certainty. His head began again to ache terribly, his eyes seemed to swim in pools of liquid fire. Bright flashes of light darted through his brain, and at times it seemed almost on fire. The pain which the constant effort to turn his head caused, was becoming more acute as each minute passed—he felt constantly on the point of screaming out in terror—begging for release—agreeing to do anything they asked of him. Then with a mighty effort of the will he would calm himself, and closing his eyes tightly once more, determine to endure until the end.

After an interminable period, the sound of the music once more fell upon his troubled brain. This time the strains sounded more distinct and clear. Three times in rapid succession *The Rosary* was played, then sudden silence. He waited in vain for more—dreading the recurrence of the song, yet expecting it, as one expects the continuance of any oft-repeated sound. There was nothing further, however, and once more the silence became like the darkness about him, a grim and positive thing.

Hours later, when his brain reeled endlessly in a blazing redness, and his tortured eyes seemed bursting from their sockets, the cone of violet light vanished as though some silent hand had brushed it aside, and in the reaction he fainted.

He awoke again to find himself lying on the floor, with Hartmann bending over him, feeling his pulse. In a fit of rage, he struck out with his clenched hand, and missing, scrambled to his feet. The room was faintly lit by the single electric globe, and he saw Mayer and Dr. Hartmann confronting him, the latter with a revolver in his hand. Once more he realized the futility of resistance, and sank against a packing box, his hand covering his burning eyes.

The latter appeared to be no longer in his former state of sardonic good nature. "Are you ready to tell us what you have done with the box?" he snarled.

Duvall made no reply, and this angered the doctor still further. "I'll give you an hour to think the matter over," he said, furiously. "And if you don't come to terms by that time, you shall stay under the influence of the light until you do." He turned toward the door, followed by Mayer, and in a moment they had left the room.

Duvall, in his pain and distress, realized that something would have to be done at once, within the next hour, in fact, or he would be obliged to give up. Physical torture he could stand, but to lie here silently, under that cruel radiance, and realize that his brain was slowly giving way, he felt he could not endure.

Yet what was there that he could do? The walls of the room, of solid brick, he could not hope to penetrate. The door, of iron, a dozen men could not break through. He forced his shoulder against it, and laughed bitterly as he realized that with all his strength he could not even cause it to give the fraction of an inch. He determined to get the snuff box—to examine it—reckless of his fear of being observed. In a moment he had snatched the opera hat from the corner, torn out the lining, and held the box in his hand.

He paused for a moment, listening intently. Everything about him was still. There were no sounds from the laboratory above. He remembered now that he had not heard Hartmann and his companion ascend the iron stairway. Doubtless they had returned to the main building by means of the lower corridor.

In a moment he had hung the torn opera hat over the knob of the door, to prevent anyone from observing him through the keyhole, and going directly beneath the bracket which held the electric globe, proceeded to examine the box carefully.

The first thought that came to his mind, filled him with a strange feeling of hope. He had no more than glanced at the top of the box when he saw what he had previously failed to observe, that the circle of pearls upon its top formed a rosary, which was completed by the ivory cross in the center. The Rosary! Why had this song been so persistently and continuously played? Was it for him, some message, indeed, intended to show him a way out of his difficulties? Yet if so, to what did it lead? There was a rosary upon the top of the box, it is true, but what of it? Absently he began to count the pearls, hardly realizing what he was doing. One of them, he noted, the one at the very top of the cross, was larger than the others, and he started here, slowly counting around the circumference of the box. His eyes pained him frightfully and twice he lost count and had to begin all over again, but on the third attempt he discovered that the pearls numbered twenty-six. Even yet, the significance of this fact did not occur to him—he began to count the pearls again, mechanically.

Then suddenly, in a flash, the thing came to him. Twenty-six pearls—twenty-six letters in the alphabet. Evidently the box, in some way, formed a cipher, a secret alphabet, which might be used in correspondence, or in the preparation of important documents, yet how—how?

With repressed eagerness he held the box more closely to the light, searching its surface for some further clue. At once he noticed the arrangement of the concentric circles of letters which made up the Latin prayer. The words were so written that each letter stood opposite a pearl, and reading inward from each pearl, there was a row of letters six deep reaching almost to the center of the box. Clearly here were six different ciphers, that is, six circles of twenty-six letters each, any one of which might constitute a working cipher. It was only necessary to call the big pearl at the top "*A*," and here were six different letters opposite it, any one of which, in a system of cipher writing, might be used as the letter *A*.

Duvall, however, knew enough about ciphers to know that such an arrangement constituted no cipher at all, in other words, that ciphers so simple, so readily solved, as this, would never be employed in any case where absolute secrecy was imperative. He felt that there was something more to the matter than he had so far discovered.

Suddenly he saw that, just beyond each pearl, was engraved on the ivory rim of the box a number—starting with the large pearl at the top as number one, the circle of numbers ran around the edge of the box until it returned to its starting point, at number twenty-six. In his efforts to see these numbers, which were very small, he gripped the box tightly in his hands to hold it the more steadily toward the rather dim light. In doing so, he suddenly became aware of the fact that the rim or edge of the box, containing the numbers and the circle of pearls, was movable. It fitted so cunningly into the top of the box, that the joint appeared not as a crack or perceptible space, but merely as a fine thin line, apparently a part of the engraving on its surface. Holding the lower part of the box firmly in his left hand, he turned the rim of the top slowly about. At once the purpose of this became apparent. Not only had each pearl, representing a letter of the alphabet, six corresponding values from rim to center, in any one position, but by turning the rim around, twenty-six such positions could be secured, making a total of one hundred and fifty-six different alphabets from which a person desiring to use a cipher might choose.

Again, however, Duvall was conscious of a feeling of disappointment. One hundred and fifty-six different ciphers were no better than a single one, if only one were used. Evidently he had not yet reached the solution of the problem. In employing such a system of ciphers, some combination, precisely similar to the combinations used on the locks of safes, would have to be used. It was absolutely necessary, in order to insure safety, to use not one cipher, but a large number, changing the arrangement of the letters with each line written—even with each word, in order to defy solution. Yet such an arrangement being purely arbitrary, could not well be trusted to memory, for, once forgotten, the translation of the document written, even by the writer himself, would be absolutely impossible. It occurred to him that as there were six different concentric lines of lettering, each constituting in itself a complete cipher, the obvious way to use the box would be to place the pearls in a given position, write six words, using a different alphabet for each word, and then shift the ring of pearls to a new position, and repeat the operation. This, of course, could be done indefinitely, although half a dozen changes would be sufficient to insure a cipher that would absolutely defy solution. Where, however, was the key? That, after all, was the important matter; without it, the snuff box would be as useless to Monsieur de Grissac as it would be to his enemies themselves.

For many minutes Duvall puzzled over the matter, unable to reach any satisfactory conclusion. Then he began to think of the song which had so clearly been repeated, over and over, as a message to him from outside. The words of the refrain began to run aimlessly through his mind, his eyes upon the box. Suddenly he realized that the word cross, in its repetitions, its position as the final word of the song, must have a definite meaning. Before his eyes he saw the cross, so delicately carved as to project scarcely an eighth of an inch above the thin and fragile ivory surface. Instinctively he began to push at it, pressing it this way and that, to discover, if possible, any spring or other means whereby it might be made to turn or lift up. As he did so, his fingers unconsciously pressed upon the large pearl at the top. In a moment the upper surface of the cross slid to one side, disclosing a tiny shallow cavity beneath it, some quarter of an inch in either direction, and no deeper than the thickness of a piece of cardboard. Within this lay a bit of tissue paper, tightly folded.

Duvall drew it carefully out and examined it. Upon it were written six numbers: 12-16-2-8-20-4. There was nothing else upon the paper, but Duvall realized that he held in his hand the key of the cipher.

At once Monsieur de Grissac's agitation, the servant Noel's death, Hartmann's persecution of him, became clear. Evidently there were documents, somewhere, of some nature, which this cipher made intelligible and which, without it, were proof against all attempts to read them. What were these documents? Were they in Hartmann's hands? These questions, he knew, could not be answered now.

Immediately the question rose in his mind: What should he do next? By destroying the tiny slip of paper, he could render the snuff box valueless. Without the key, no one could use it with success. But, the key once destroyed, how could Monsieur de Grissac himself read the documents, for the preparing of which it had been utilized? Possibly, if Hartmann had such documents, they were but copies, obtained through the corruption of some clerk, while the originals remained in De Grissac's possession. For these reasons he dared not destroy the cipher, at least until all other means of escape had been exhausted. Then he realized, in a flash, that if he proposed to utilize the return of the snuff box as a means of obtaining his freedom, he could not hope to do so, if the key was removed. Doubtless Hartmann knew of its existence. In some way he had learned, possibly through the murdered man Noel, that the box contained such a key, and would examine it, and satisfy himself that it had not been removed, before he would allow him to leave the place. This would inevitably result in his being searched, and the key, concealed about his person, found. He stood in an agony of doubt, wondering which alternative he should take.

His reflections were rudely disturbed by the sound of footsteps in the corridor outside the door. In a moment he had replaced the tiny bit of paper in the recess beneath the cross, slid the latter back into place, and thrust the box beneath a mass of straw which lay on top of the packing case against which he had been leaning. Then he turned toward the door and had barely time to hurl the opera hat into a dark corner, when the door opened, and Hartmann appeared on the threshold.

CHAPTER XIX

It was not until early in the afternoon that Grace was able to accomplish anything toward carrying out the instructions which young Lablanche had given her with respect to the phonograph. On her return to Dr. Hartmann's from her expedition to Brussels, she went at once to her room, and locked the record which Lablanche had given her in her trunk. There was nothing to be done now, until after luncheon.

When the meal was over, she asked one of the attendants, who seemed to be a sort of housekeeper, or head nurse, if there would be any objection to her taking the phonograph, which was a small and rather cheap affair, to her room. She wished to amuse herself, she explained, playing over some of the records.

The woman regarded her curiously for a moment, but as there seemed nothing out of the way in the request, she assented, with the caution, however, that she should not use the instrument except during the day. "Some of our patients are very nervous," she explained. "It might annoy them, if they were sleeping. Of course, if there are any complaints, you will not continue."

Grace got one of the nurses to carry the instrument to her room, and selected several records from those which she found in a cabinet on which it stood. There were several American records—she took all of these, and some others selected at random.

She did not play The Rosary at once, but made use of one of the other records. The horn of the instrument she directed toward the open window. When she had finished the first air, and adjusted her own record upon the plate of the machine, she felt afraid that it might at once be recognized as strange and new, but apparently no one paid any attention to it.

She continued her playing as long as she dared without running the risk of attracting undue attention. When at last she stopped, she felt as though she never wanted to hear the strains of The Rosary again.

After dinner, she determined to disregard the suggestion of the housekeeper to confine her playing to the daytime, and moving the machine somewhat nearer the window, played the song over three times in rapid succession. She had just begun to rewind the clockwork for a fourth time when there was a loud knocking at the door, and Dr. Hartmann entered hastily in response to her rather frightened "Come in."

He was scowling fiercely, and took no pains to conceal the fact that he was angry. "Miss Ellicott," he growled, "we cannot possibly permit you to play the instrument any longer. It annoys the other patients. I am surprised that my housekeeper did not inform you so at once. Several have already complained. I shall have to take it back to the library." He gathered up the instrument and started toward the door, then seemed for a moment to regret his brusqueness. "You will pardon me, I know, but it is quite out of the question. Good-evening." In a moment he had gone.

Grace sat down and burst into tears. It was not the taking away of the phonograph which distressed her—she felt that if anything could be accomplished by its use, it had already been done—but the hopelessness of the whole situation.

Nearly eighteen hours had elapsed, since she had stolen, half-fainting, from the sight of Richard's white and agonized face. Even Lablanche's assurances that Hartmann would do her husband no serious injury, failed to comfort her. The whole affair of the phonograph seemed trivial and useless. What message could the words of this song give him—what in fact could they mean to anyone, except a message of hopeless love?

When the hour for going to bed had come, she threw herself, without undressing, on the bed, and lay sleepless, in the darkened room. The vision of Richard, as she had seen him, his face within the circle of light, the night before, tortured her incessantly. It seemed somehow so wrong, so cowardly of her, to lie here in comfort doing nothing to aid him who, in name at least, was united to her forever, and in love was more dear to her than her own soul. She could not sleep, and presently rose and sat at the window, her elbows resting upon the sill, gazing hungrily out at the little square brick building where she knew Richard lay confined.

The hours of the night dragged along on leaden feet. Once she heard the closing of a door, and the sound of footsteps echoing faintly upon the cement floor of the lower corridor. Within the laboratory all seemed dark. Evidently the doctor was not there. Then she heard, through her half-opened door, noises of persons walking in the lower hallway of the main building and after that the sharp closing of a door. She concluded that Hartmann had gone into his office.

The woman on duty in the hall sat in her chair, reading and yawning. After a time, Grace heard the faint ringing of her bell, and the woman, after consulting the indicator, began to descend the stairs with a surprised look upon her face. It seemed like a providential opportunity. She slipped quietly through the doorway and sped as swiftly as she could down the hall.

She reached the door opening into the corridor, without hearing or seeing anything to cause her alarm, and passed through it unseen. As she closed it behind her, she fancied she heard someone walking quickly along the corridor beneath. The passageway in which she stood was in reality nothing but a covered bridge, a few feet wide, built for the sole purpose of providing a means of passing to the laboratory from the second floor of the main building. Beneath it, a similar passageway connected the ground floors of the two buildings.

She realized that anyone in the corridor beneath her could readily hear her footsteps on the wooden floor above, and stood, hesitating, just inside the door, waiting until they should have passed. In a few moments, the sounds below ceased, and silence again reigned.

With great timidity and caution, she began to walk toward the laboratory door. In the center of the corridor, and half way down its length, a single electric lamp shed a dim light on her path. She realized that if, by chance, anyone should be within the darkened laboratory, they could readily see her approaching, and therefore assumed once more the manner and bearing of a person walking in their sleep. She had passed the light in the middle of the corridor, and was nearing the darkened laboratory door, when suddenly she heard a faint click, and almost at once the laboratory was brilliantly illuminated.

By the light which suddenly flashed upon her, she saw two figures standing in the open door of the laboratory, watching her intently. One of these figures was Dr. Hartmann, the other the tall blond man she had seen with him in the laboratory several nights before. But it was not the sudden appearance of the two watching figures which caused her heart to sink, and a cold perspiration to break out upon her forehead. The sudden rush of light upon the floor of the passageway had shown her something else—something far more strange and terrifying. As her gaze swept ahead, she saw that, for a space of some four or five feet, in front of the laboratory door, the wooden planking which constituted the floor of the passageway had been removed, and instead of the solid foot-way there yawned blackly an impassable opening, through which, in another moment, she would plunge headlong to the concrete floor of the corridor beneath.

The sight filled her with dismay. She realized at once why Hartmann and his companion stood there watching her—why the section of flooring had been removed. He had evidently become suspicious of her movements, the night before, and had laid this trap to test her. If she was in truth walking in her sleep, she would, she supposed, walk fearlessly into the yawning gap before—if her somnambulism was a sham, a trick, she would hesitate, and her fraud be discovered.

She did not know what to do, as step by step she approached that black and gaping hole. If she kept up her pretense, if she had sufficient courage to go ahead, of what would it avail Richard or Monsieur Lefevre, should she maintain her assumed character at the expense of a broken leg, or neck? On the other hand, to halt, to hold back, would be to destroy at once all chance of her being of any further service to her husband, and that, too, at a time when he most sorely needed her.

These considerations flashed through her brain with the speed of light itself. She had scarcely taken half a dozen steps before she found herself upon the brink of the opening, and realized that the next step, if she took it, might be her last.

Then she suddenly collapsed. The effort was too great—she sank helplessly upon the floor, her face buried in her arms, her whole body shaking with the force of her sobbing.

In an instant Hartmann had sprung across the opening and grasped her by the wrist, while his companion was engaged in rapidly replacing over the gap the section of flooring which had been removed. Within a few moments the passageway was as it had been before, and the doctor was dragging her roughly into the laboratory.

She did not cry out—there was no one from whom she could expect aid. She drew herself up and faced her captor with dry eyes and a face calm, though pale. "What do you mean, Dr. Hartmann," she demanded, steadily, "by treating me in this way?"

He forced her into a chair. "Sit down, young woman," he said, gruffly. "I have a few questions to ask you."

She did so, without protest, summoning to her aid all her powers of resistance and will. He should get nothing from her, she determined.

"Why have you come into my house," he presently asked, glaring at her in anger, "under pretense of desiring medical treatment? What is it you want here?"

She made no reply, gazing at him steadily—fearlessly.

"What is this man Duvall to you?" he shouted. "Tell me, or it will be the worse for you both."

Again she faced him, refusing to answer. Her resistance made him furious. "Your silence will profit you nothing," he went on. "You can do no further harm here, for I know your purpose. You are working with him—you are a detective—a spy, as he is. You pretend to be a somnambulist in order to carry out your ends. I suspected you long ago. Now I know. This man has robbed me of something that I am determined to have. What he has done with it—where it is concealed, I do not know, but I mean to have it—be sure of that. If you know—you had better confess, if you have any regard for his welfare."

His words, his brutal manner, brought the tears to her eyes. She realized that she had but to say a few words, to save Richard from she knew not what fate, yet equally she knew that she could not say them—that he would not want her to say them. In her agitation she took a handkerchief from her dress and pressed it to her eyes.

The man Mayer had been regarding her in silence throughout the whole scene. Suddenly he stepped forward and snatched the handkerchief from her hand. His quick eyes had detected a monogram in one corner of the bit of cambric, and with an air of triumph he held it beneath the light, examining it closely.

Hartmann came to him. "What is it, Mayer?" he asked, eagerly.

His assistant extended the handkerchief to him. Grace realized with a sinking heart that it was one of several she had herself embroidered during the weeks preceding her marriage. With what pride, she reflected, she had worked over the G and D, lovingly intertwined in one corner. "His wife!" she heard Hartmann cry, with a harsh laugh. "That explains everything. That was why he did not leave Brussels at once—he was waiting for her— he would not go without her." He turned to Grace with a new expression on his face. "So you are his wife, eh? Very well. Now we shall see whether or not you will tell me what I want to know. Your husband is confined in the room below us. This"—he indicated the small black box with wires attached—"is a device which I have constructed for producing certain light rays—light rays which have a marvelous power, both for curing, and producing disease. Look!" He held his powerful hand before her eyes. "This is what they did to me, before I discovered how to control them." She saw, stretching across the back of his hand and wrist, a broad red patch, like the scar remaining after a burn. "Now come here." He seized her by the wrist and dragged her toward the apparatus at the center of the room. "Look—in there." He indicated a short brass tube which rose from the center of the box, resembling the eyepiece of a microscope. "Look!"

Grace bent over and applied her eye to the brass tube, then shrank back with an exclamation of horror. "Richard!" she screamed, then turned on Hartmann with the fury of a tigress. "Let him go—let him go—I say, or I will—" She realized her helplessness—the futility of her threats, and fell into the chair in a paroxysm of sobbing. Through the brass tube, and the powerful lens which focused the light rays upon the space below, she had seen Richard's face, white and drawn, within a disk of blinding light, and apparently so near to her that she could have reached out and touched it. In her momentary glance, she noted his reddened eyes, the tears which coursed from beneath their lids, the agony which distorted his countenance.

"Now will you tell me what I ask?" cried Hartmann, triumphantly.

Still she made no reply. Her heart was breaking, her suffering at the knowledge of his suffering made her faint and weak, but even now she could not bring herself to break the trust which Monsieur Lefevre had placed in her. She sat huddled up in the chair, shaking from head to foot with sobs.

Hartmann saw that her resistance was as yet unbroken. "Take her arm, Mayer," he called out, as he seized her by one wrist. "Come along now. We'll see if a closer view will have any effect." He snatched up a broad leather strap from a shelf along the wall, then, with Mayer's assistance, half-led, half dragged her to the iron stairway in the corner. In a few moments they had paused before the door of the room where the detective lay confined. Hartmann threw it open and pushed Grace inside, while he and Mayer followed, closing the door behind them.

For a moment Grace was dazzled by the brightness of the light cone, and the darkness of the remainder of the room. Then seeing Richard lying helpless on the floor before her, she threw herself to her knees, put her arms about his neck, and covered his face with kisses. "My darling—my poor boy!" she cried, as she bent over him, her shoulders shutting off from his tortured face the blinding rays of the light. "What have they done to you?"

Chapter XX

Grace had remained upon her knees beside the prostrate figure of her husband but a moment, when she was torn away by Hartmann and his assistant, and before she realized their intention, the former had slipped about her waist the broad leather strap he had brought from the room above, and was busy securing it to an iron staple fixed in the wall at one side of the room. Then he stood back and surveyed the scene with a smile of satisfaction.

"You see, Mayer," he observed, grimly, "my purpose. The wife sees the husband's suffering. If he refuses to speak, she will speak. One or the other will tell us what we want to know, of that you may be sure. Let us leave them to talk matters over." He and his man at once left the room, and in a few moments Grace heard their footsteps upon the floor of the laboratory above.

"Richard," she cried, softly, "are you suffering very much?"

"Never mind, dear," he said, trying vainly to turn his head so that he might see her. "What has happened—why have they brought you here?"

She told him her story, brokenly, with many sobs. "I could not help it, Richard," she moaned. "I did my best. I could not help their finding out everything."

"I know it, dear. You have done all you could. Is there any news from outside?"

"None. They told me to play the phonograph to send you a message. Did you hear it?"

"Yes, I heard, and understood."

"Understood? Then you know something—you have some hope?"

"I do not know. It may be, although I cannot see what to do now. I dare not tell you more than that—these scoundrels are undoubtedly listening in the room above."

"Richard, what is that light? What is it they mean to do to you? Dr. Hartmann showed me his hand—it was all scarred and burned. He said it came from that." She looked toward the glowing cone of light with bitter anger.

"I do not know—exactly. I am not sure. The agony of the thing is very great—it burns into my eyes—into my brain. Hartmann says it will produce insanity. I do not know whether this is true or not. I begin to feel that perhaps it may be—not that the light itself can produce it, but that inability to sleep, pain, nervous exhaustion, the constant glare and brilliance before my eyes—those things might cause a man to go insane, if they were kept up long enough."

"But—he—he will not dare to do that."

Duvall groaned, striving in vain to turn his head to one side. "He intends to keep me here, until I tell him where he can find the snuff box," he gasped.

"Richard!" Grace fairly screamed out his name. "Then you must tell—you *must*! You cannot let yourself go mad—not even for Monsieur Lefevre."

"I shall not tell—no matter what comes," he replied.

"Then *I* will. I refuse to let you suffer like this. I can't do it, I won't. If you do not speak, I shall. Oh, my God! Don't you see—I love you—I love you so—what do I care about this foolish snuff box? I want you—you—and I *won't* let them take you away from me."

"Grace, you shall not tell them."

"I will."

"I forbid it."

"I cannot help it, Richard. I am ready to disobey you— if I must, to save your life. Even if you turn from me— afterward—I cannot help it. I refuse to let them go ahead with this thing."

He groaned in desperation. "Please—please—my girl—listen to me. You must not speak. We must think of our duty to those who have trusted us. Wait, I implore you. Don't do this!"

"I will. I have a duty to you which is greater than my duty to them. Dr. Hartmann!" she screamed. "I will tell everything—everything." She collapsed against the wall and sobbed as though her heart would break.

In a few moments they heard Hartmann and Mayer descending the steps, and the door was thrown open.

"Ah, so you have come to your senses, have you?" the doctor cried. "Well, what have you to say?"

Grace raised her head. "If I tell you where the ivory snuff box is hidden," she said, "will you let my husband go?"

"Yes. Your husband, and yourself, and the rat we've just caught sneaking around outside. He's up in the laboratory now. You can all take yourselves off as quickly as you like, when once the snuff box is in my hands. Now speak."

"First, let my husband up."

Hartmann went to the wall, and switching off the violet rays, turned on the electric lamp, then nodded to Mayer. "Unbind him," he said.

Duvall staggered to his feet, half-blinded. As he did so, Hartmann turned to Grace. "Speak!" he commanded. "We are wasting time."

Before Grace could reply, Duvall turned to her.

"I forbid you," he cried. "If you do this thing, I will never see you again as long as I live. You are destroying my honor. I refuse to let you do it. Stop!"

The girl hesitated, and Hartmann swore a great oath. "Take her out of here, Mayer," he cried. "She'll never speak, as long as her husband is present to dissuade her. Up with her to the laboratory. She'll talk there, quick enough."

"No!" Duvall staggered toward her. "You shall not." His movements were slow and uncertain, due to the blinding pain in his eyes, and his stiffened, nerve-racked limbs. Hartmann pushed him aside angrily. "Be quiet," he growled. "Let the woman alone."

Meanwhile Hartmann's companion had torn away the strap which bound Grace to the wall and was leading her to the door. Her husband's efforts to detain her, weak and uncertain, were easily frustrated by Hartmann. In a few moments the door had swung shut upon the detective, and she was being led up the steps to the room above.

Here she fell into a chair, and looking about, saw huddled on a couch in the far corner of the room a little, bent old man, who sat with his white head bowed upon his breast, his hands tied behind his back. Hartmann went over to him and unfastened his bonds. "You will be happier in a moment, my friend," he laughed. "This lady is going to set you free."

Dufrenne—for it was he—sprang to his feet. "How?" he demanded. "How?" As he spoke, he crossed the room, his eyes gleaming, and faced Grace as she sat in the chair.

"Wait and see, old man," said Hartmann, roughly. "Stand aside, please." He pushed Dufrenne impatiently away. "Now, young woman, where is the ivory snuff box?"

Grace raised her head to reply, when the little old Frenchman turned to her, pale with anger. "No!" he shouted, starting forward. "You shall not do this thing. Would you be a traitor to France!"

Grace looked at him and shuddered. His face was quivering with emotion—his eyes burned with piercing brightness, he seemed about to spring at her, in his rage. In a moment Hartmann had turned on him. "Be quiet!" he roared. "I want no interference from you. Mayer!" He pointed a trembling forefinger at the old Frenchman. "Take this fellow away."

Mayer took Dufrenne by the arm and twisted it cruelly. "No nonsense, now!" he growled, thrusting the old man toward the couch upon which he had been sitting. "Hold your tongue, or it will be worse for you." Dufrenne resisted him as best he could, but his age and feebleness rendered him helpless. He sank upon the couch, with tears of anger starting to his eyes.

Grace dared not look at him. The enormity of the thing she was about to do appalled her. Yet there was Richard, her husband; Richard, whom she loved with all her soul, in the room below, facing madness, death. The love she felt for him overmastered all other considerations. She turned to Hartmann with quivering face. "The box is in the room below," she cried, in a voice shaking with emotion.

"*Mon Dieu—mon Dieu!*" she heard Dufrenne gasp, as he started from the couch. "You have ruined us all."

Hartmann and Mayer gazed at each other incredulously. "Impossible!" the former gasped. "Impossible!" Then he turned to Grace. "Girl, are you telling me the truth?"

She nodded, bowing her head upon her hands. She could not trust herself to speak.

"Where? Where in that room could it be hidden? Tell me!" he shook her angrily by the arm. "Haven't we wasted enough time over this thing?"

Still she made no reply. Now that she had told them, a sudden revulsion swept over her. She hated herself for what she had done, hated Hartmann, hated Monsieur Lefevre for placing her in this cruel situation.

Hartmann dragged her roughly to her feet. "If the box is in the room below, come with me and find it."

He hurried her toward the staircase. "Come along, Mayer," he called over his shoulder. "Bring that fellow with you. It won't be safe to leave him." As she descended the steps, Grace heard the other two close behind her. The Frenchman staggered along like a man in a daze, offering no resistance.

When they burst into the room in which Duvall was confined, they found the latter standing beneath the electric lamp, a look of determination upon his face. He regarded them steadily, in spite of his reddened and burning eyes.

Hartmann paid little attention to him. He was too greatly interested in the movements of Grace. "Now," he said, "where is it? You say the snuff box is here—in this room. Find it."

She hesitated, looking at her husband pitifully. What would he think of her? Would he, too, regard her as a traitor, a weak and contemptible creature, forever barred from love and respect, false to her duty, her honor? His face told her nothing. He was regarding her impassively. She remembered now that he had said that he would never see her again if she disobeyed him. Then she turned away, her mind made up. She would save him, come what might. He had told her that the box was hidden in an opera hat, in one corner of the room. She glanced about quickly, trying to discover its whereabouts in one of the dark corners.

Duvall saw her intention. He took a step forward, and addressed Hartmann. "You have forced this girl, through her love for me, to betray a great trust. I prefer that, if anyone here is to become a traitor, it shall be myself." He thrust his hand into the pocket of his coat, and extended a round white object toward the astonished doctor. "Here is the snuff box."

Dufrenne, for the moment left unguarded by Mayer, sprang forward with a fierce cry. "No—no—no!" he screamed. "You shall not—you shall not."

"Out of my way!" exclaimed the doctor, brushing the old man aside as easily as though the latter had been a child. With eager hands he took the box, and going to the light, bent over it. As he saw the pearls, the cross, his face lit up with delight. "This is it, Mayer. Just as the valet described it." He gave the ring of pearls a swift turn, then pressed immediately upon the larger one of the circle and slid the top of the ivory cross to one side. Duvall, who was watching him with interest, concluded that from some source, probably through Monsieur de Grissac's dead servant, Dr. Hartmann had learned thoroughly the secret of the box.

With a cry of satisfaction the latter drew out from the tiny recess the slip of folded paper, glanced at the row of numbers written upon it, then passed it over to Mayer. The latter nodded his head. "Now we are all right," he muttered. "This is easily worth a million francs."

"Money doesn't measure its value, my friend," the doctor remarked, gravely, as he replaced the slip of paper beneath the cross and put the box carefully into his pocket.

During these few moments, Dufrenne had been observing the doctor with bulging eyes. Suddenly he turned on the detective. "May the good God curse you and your woman for this," he cried, hoarsely, "until the day of your death. May He turn all men against you, and make your name a despised and dishonored one forever. You have been false to your duty—false to France. You are a traitor, a contemptible dog of a traitor, and you deserve to die." His whole body shook with passion as he poured the fury of his wrath upon the man before him.

Duvall sank weakly against the packing case behind him. Suffering, lack of sleep and food, the burning pain in his eyes and brain, threatened to overcome him. "Let me alone," he gasped. "I am so tired, so very tired!" He almost fell as he uttered the words and indeed would have done so had Grace not gone quickly up to him and passed her arm lovingly about his shoulders. Turning to Dufrenne, she regarded him with a look of defiance. "He is not guilty!" she cried. "It is I—I!—who have been false. I made him do it—I made him do it. Go away, and tell the others what you please. I know that my husband has done his best." She fell to soothing him, kissing him upon his hot forehead, his burning cheeks.

Dufrenne looked at Dr. Hartmann, who was regarding the scene before him with impatience. "Do I understand, monsieur," he asked, in a ghastly voice, "that I am free to leave this place?"

"Yes. Out with you. I could hold you for trespass upon my grounds, for attempting to break into my house, but I don't want to be bothered with you. Go!" He went to the door and held it open. "Mayer," he said, "show this fellow the road. And as for you"—he turned to Duvall and his wife—"get away from here, and from Brussels, as soon as you like. I advise you not to stay in the town. I rather think that, through the evidence of Seltz, I can make it slightly uncomfortable for you. Tell what story you please. I have done you no injury. You came here of your own free will—you could have escaped and you would not. As for the light—" He laughed harshly. "An ordinary arc, focused on your eyes with a powerful lens. It would probably have blinded you, in time, and if it kept you awake long enough, you would no doubt have gone mad, but so far you are not hurt much. I can swear that it is part of my new treatment for a disordered mental state. My man here will agree with me. What are you going to do about it? How are you going to explain your robbery of Seltz in my office, the deception your wife has practised upon me and upon the United States Minister? And above all, now that I have the secret I desired, I am quite willing to have a cast made of the snuff box and return it to you, but I fancy that neither Monsieur de Grissac nor my friend Lefevre will want to have the matter made public in the courts. You'd better leave here quietly and take the first steamer to America. I don't fancy you'll find a very flattering reception awaiting you in Paris." He turned to the door. "Come, I'll have your belongings put on a cab, and be glad to be rid of you." He paused beside the doorway, waiting.

Grace turned to her husband. "Come, Richard," she said. "Let us go."

He made no reply, but followed her blindly. His spirits seemed broken, he walked like a man in a heavy sleep.

It was just dawn when, half an hour later, Richard Duvall and his wife drove silently through the ghostly streets of Brussels toward the railway station. The detective did not speak. He sat silent, plunged in a deep stupor. Grace, her heart breaking, held one of his hands, and with white face, gazed helplessly out of the window at the city, just waking to another day. To all these people the dawn came with some measure of hope, of happiness, but to her, and to her husband, now once more beginning their honeymoon, the future seemed full of bitterness and despair. She shivered in the cold morning air, and the tears she could not repress stole unheeded down her cheeks.

CHAPTER XXI

It was not until they had reached the railway station that Richard Duvall roused himself from the stupor in which he had sat ever since he and his wife had driven away from Dr. Hartmann's. When their baggage had been deposited on the platform, under the care of a solicitous porter, and the cabman had been paid and gone his way, Grace asked her husband concerning their destination. "Shall we go to Antwerp?" she said, listlessly. "We can get a steamer there, or cross to England." She awaited his reply without interest. It seemed to matter very little where they went, now.

Duvall turned to the waiting porter. "When is the next train for Paris?" he asked. The man answered at once, glancing at the clock in the waiting-room. "In forty minutes, monsieur. You will have time for rolls and coffee."

"Paris!" exclaimed Grace, in much surprise. "Why should we go to Paris, dear? I don't care about the things I left there. We can telegraph for them. Oh, Richard, I can't go back and face Monsieur Lefevre now." She looked eagerly at his face, but its expression told her nothing. "I must make my report to the Prefect," he answered. "It is my duty."

Over their simple breakfast he was uncommunicative. "Don't worry, dear," he said, once, when she had plied him with questions, attempted to change his decision by arguments. "I cannot afford to run away. Monsieur Lefevre has given me a duty to perform, and I must at least tell my story. After that, we can go to America, but not now."

She could get no more out of him, and with tears in her eyes, followed him to the compartment in the Paris train which the porter had secured for them. There were few people traveling at this early hour. They had the compartment to themselves. Duvall rolled himself in his overcoat and lay down upon one of the seats. "I am very tired, dear," he told her. "I have suffered a frightful strain. My eyes hurt so that I can scarcely see. I am sick for want of sleep. There is a hard task before me, when I get to Paris. I must have a little rest." He turned his face away from the light, and lay quiet, breathing heavily.

Grace sat huddled up in a corner of the opposite seat, watching him, a great tenderness in her eyes. After all, she thought, he was her husband, the man she loved, and if he had appeared to act the part of a traitor to his cause, it was only because she, by her weakness, her love for him, had forced him to do so. At the last moment he had thought of her—his one thought had been to save her from disgrace and dishonor. He had assumed the blame, for he had given up the snuff box of his own free will. Had he allowed her to do so, he could have preserved his own name, his own honor, clear of all accusation or stain. It made her love him doubly, that he had thus stepped into the breach at the last moment and taken upon himself the guilt which she knew belonged in reality upon her.

As she sat there, conscious only of the flying trees outside the car windows, the clicking of the wheels upon the rails, and the low breathing of her husband on the seat before her, her mind went forward into the future, and the prospect made her shudder. In Paris she knew what manner of welcome awaited them. Monsieur Lefevre would turn from them both, as he would not turn from the vilest criminal.

Their names would be held up to scorn, in official circles at least. If the public ever came to know of the affair, she knew they would have reason to fear for their very safety.

As to the results of her act, as to what the secret of the lost snuff box was, that made Hartmann declare its value to be priceless, she could not even guess. That it must have some diplomatic, some international significance, she fully believed, else why should Monsieur Lefevre have declared that the honor of France was involved? And if so—if the possession of the secret by Hartmann, and thus by the foreign country, whichever one it might be, of which he was probably an agent, did result in complications of a vast and terrible nature, involving possibly war, or loss of national honor and prestige, how could either she or her husband ever again hope to hold up their heads, to find any joy and happiness in life?

Of course, there was America, and home, but even there the secret would in time become known, and Richard would find that those who had been his friends in high places would turn from him, trusting in his honor, his integrity, no longer. Even, she realized, if the affair did not become known, at home, it would stand forever between them, a black and grinning shadow, destroying confidence, happiness, even love itself. She had failed him—failed her husband—done what he had forbidden her to do, and he had sworn to leave her, to turn from her forever, if she disobeyed him. Would he do this, she wondered? Or would he understand that what she had done, had been for his sake, for the sake of her love for him?

Presently she realized that the train was slackening its speed, and the houses which began to appear in increasing numbers outside the car windows told her that they were approaching a station. She looked at her railway folder and then consulted her watch. It was Manbenge, the point at which they left Belgium and entered France. The train drew noisily into the station, and was at once surrounded by the usual crowd of passengers, porters, railway and customs officials, and the like. Grace watched them idly, indifferently. Her only concern was that they should not wake her husband with their noisy chatter.

Presently she saw a small, white-haired figure approaching the compartment door. At first she paid no attention to the man, supposing him to be a belated passenger. Then she was struck with a sudden familiarity in his appearance. She started back in alarm as she saw that it was Dufrenne, and that he was making straight for the compartment in which she sat, his face stern and angry. Behind him she observed two gendarmes, walking with their characteristic jerky stride.

Dufrenne had been a mystery to her. Until their meeting in Dr. Hartmann's laboratory that morning, she had never seen him. She had felt, from his words, that he, too, was of Monsieur Lefevre's staff, a member of the secret police, but that he was no friend of Richard's or of hers, she very well knew. She drew back further into the dim corner of the compartment, hoping that he would not recognize her.

Her hopes, however, were in vain. Dufrenne threw open the door of the carriage, which had previously been unlocked by the guard, and followed by his men, entered the compartment. "Here is the fellow," he cried, angrily, pointing to Duvall. "Arrest him."

Grace sprang forward, and stood between the men and her husband, who slept on, unconscious of the noise about him. "No—no!" she cried, in a tense whisper. "Let him alone. You shall not touch him." In her desperation she drew from the bosom of her dress a small revolver which she had carried ever since she left Paris. "Keep away, I tell you. You shall not arrest my husband."

Dufrenne confronted her with an angry gesture. "You fool!" he cried. "Do you dare to disobey this?" He held before her eyes a silver ring, inlaid with gold, similar to the one she wore about her own neck. "I am a member of the secret police, as you know. This man is a traitor to his duty, and for that he shall be punished. Arrest him," he said again to his men.

Grace recoiled, and dropped the revolver she held to the floor. In all her dread of the future, this was something upon which she had not counted. Her husband arrested—possibly shot, or condemned to spend years in some frightful military prison. She thought of Devil's Island, where Dreyfus had been confined, and the horror of the situation overcame her. Unable to resist longer, she sank upon the seat and burst into tears.

The two gendarmes awakened Duvall roughly, and after informing him that he was a prisoner, sat grimly down on either side of him. Dufrenne took the seat beside Grace. The train had again begun to move—she realized that they were once more flying toward Paris.

At first Duvall, in his stupor of sleep, did not realize what had happened, but in a few moments he had grasped the situation. He did not seem greatly concerned at his arrest, and Grace, her first paroxysm of weeping having passed, looked at him in surprise. How brave he is! she thought. Once she caught his eyes, but he made no sign. Apparently he was resigned to his fate.

Dufrenne turned to her presently. "You, madame, are also under arrest," he remarked coldly.

"You have no right to do this thing," she exclaimed. "We have done the best we could."

"No!" cried the little old Frenchman, his bent shoulders straightening, his eyes flashing until he became a stern and vengeful figure. "No! You have not done the best you could. Brave men—and brave women, die at their posts of duty. You are cowards, both of you. Had I been in your place, do you think I would have given in—do you think I would have sold the honor of my country! *Mon Dieu!* It is incredible! I am a Frenchman, madame, and I have fought for France. I value my life as nothing, where her welfare is concerned. I would have died a thousand times, died as Frenchmen die, with '*Vive La France*,' on my lips, before I would have uttered so much as a single word."

She made no reply to this. In his anger, the fragile old man seemed inspired with the very spirit of patriotism, his withered cheeks took on new color, his sunken eyes a new brightness. She felt ashamed—not for Richard, for he had spoken only when she had forced him to do so, but for herself. The guilt was hers. She was glad that she, too, was arrested, that she might have a chance to go before Monsieur Lefevre and take upon her shoulders the dishonor which she knew belonged there. Silent, she shrank back into her corner, not daring to look up.

"Monsieur Dufrenne," she heard Richard saying, quietly, "be so good as to remember that it was I, not my wife, who gave the snuff box to Hartmann. You have seen fit to place me under arrest. Very well, I will tell my story to Monsieur Lefevre and abide by his decision. But meanwhile, I beg that you will treat my wife with courtesy and respect. She has had a very trying and terrible experience and I do not wonder that she is unnerved. You may not know it, monsieur, but we were married but five days ago, and this—" he glanced about the compartment with a sad smile—"this, monsieur, is our honeymoon."

The Frenchman sank back, all his anger swept away. "It is pitiful, monsieur, pitiful," he said, quietly. "Yet in what I now do, I am but doing my duty." He turned to Grace. "Madame, I feel for you in your suffering. You acted through love. Of that I am sure. But there is a greater love than that of woman for man—the love of country. That is the only love I understand." He turned away and sat for a long while gazing out of the window.

In what seemed to Grace a very short time, they reached Paris, and here she and Richard were conducted to a taxicab and soon found themselves at the Prefecture.

Dufrenne left them, to announce his arrival to Monsieur Lefevre, and she and her husband sat in an anteroom, closely guarded, waiting until the time should arrive for them to be summoned before the Prefect.

The detective was still silent and preoccupied. He said little, but from the caressing way in which he placed his hand upon hers, bidding her cheer up, Grace knew that his love for her, at least, was left to her. "Oh, Richard," she said, softly, turning her face to his, "I am so sorry, so sorry! But I could not let you suffer, dear, for I love you— I love you."

CHAPTER XXII

It was characteristic of Monsieur Etienne Lefevre, Prefect of Police of Paris, that when he had once placed a case in the hands of one of his men, he rarely ever interfered in any way with the latter's conduct of it. Reports of progress he did not desire, nor encourage. Success was the only report that he asked, and by thus throwing his subordinates upon their own responsibility, he obtained from them far better results than would have been the case had he kept in constant touch with their movements.

Hence when he dispatched Richard Duvall, and Monsieur Dufrenne, the little curio dealer of the *Rue de Richelieu*, to London, and the former's wife and later on Lablanche to Brussels, he felt that he had done all that it was possible to do, to secure the recovery of Monsieur de Grissac's stolen snuff box.

He did not, it is true, dismiss the matter from his mind—it was, indeed, of too grave and sinister a character to be treated thus lightly, but he had the utmost confidence in Duvall, and believed that the latter would without doubt succeed in his quest.

Since Duvall's departure, he had waited anxiously for the detective's appearance. He did not expect to hear from him, but felt convinced that within the next day or two he would walk into his office with the missing snuff box in his pocket.

It was with some dismay, therefore, that he received, on the fourth day, a sudden visit from Dufrenne. The latter had been released, the day before, by the Brussels police, after a most uncomfortable night in a cell, an experience for which he knew he had Hartmann to thank, and in desperation had decided to place the condition of affairs before his chief.

The latter had heard him in silence, and then followed a long conference, with the result that Dufrenne returned to Brussels, bearing the mysterious message subsequently given to Grace by Lablanche, to play *The Rosary* upon the phonograph.

Since then, the Prefect had been in a state of profound agitation, although he carefully concealed the fact from his subordinates. The gravity of the issues at stake tortured him ceaselessly, and to add to his discomfort, Monsieur de Grissac arrived from London, determined to ascertain what progress, if any, had been made toward the recovery of his lost property.

He was bitterly disappointed to find that Lefevre was unable to give him the slightest encouragement. The box had not, he believed, passed into the hands of their enemies, but beyond that he could say nothing.

It was on the day of the Ambassador's arrival that Dufrenne appeared at the Prefecture a second time, his face pale and haggard, his eyes bloodshot and sunken from loss of sleep, his whole manner indicating that he had lately passed through some terrible experience. De Grissac was closeted with the Prefect at the time, but the man's appearance, his urgent request that he see Monsieur Lefevre at once, gained him an immediate audience.

The Prefect and the Ambassador stood awaiting his entrance, their faces tense with anxiety. The expression upon the old man's countenance confirmed their worst fears. He staggered into the room, grasping the back of a chair to support himself. "He has given it up—the scoundrel—the traitor; he has given it up, to save himself and his wife."

The Ambassador turned away with a groan of despair. Lefevre stepped up to Dufrenne. "You mean to tell me," he cried, "that Richard Duvall has proven false to his duty? I cannot believe it."

Dufrenne nodded. "He gave it to Hartmann last night. I saw him do it. Hartmann had promised to let him go free. They had been torturing him, in some way, I do not know how. It was the woman who weakened first. The man—Duvall—gave up the box to save her from doing so."

"Then she knew where it was?"

"Yes."

The Prefect went over to the window and looked out over the Seine. His emotions almost overcame him. The loss of the box—Duvall's faithlessness—his own failure, all plunged him into the deepest despair. "*Mon Dieu!*" he muttered to himself. "Duvall—it is incredible!"

Suddenly he turned. The Ambassador had begun to question Dufrenne. "What did this Dr. Hartmann do, when the box was given to him?" he asked in a voice trembling with excitement.

"He pressed the large pearl, pushed aside the cross, and removed the paper that was hidden beneath it. He read the paper. It contained nothing but a row of numbers. I saw it as he held it beneath the light."

De Grissac became as white as chalk, and turning to Lefevre, cried out, in a broken voice, "It is all over. Nothing can be done now. It is too late. *Mon Dieu!* What will become of France?"

"Where is Duvall?" cried the Prefect, suddenly. "I must see him. He is not the man to do such a thing as this. I must talk to him. Do not tell me that he has run away."

"No, monsieur. He is outside, he and his wife. I have placed them both under arrest."

"Were they attempting to escape?"

"No, monsieur. They were coming to Paris."

"At least," the Prefect remarked, mournfully, "he is not cowardly enough for that. Bring him here—bring them both here at once. I must question them."

Dufrenne turned to the door. "In a moment, monsieur, they will be before you."

"What can it avail now?" said De Grissac, sadly.

"We shall see. I never condemn a man without a hearing." As he spoke, Duvall and Grace came into the room.

The Prefect looked at his young assistant with an expression both grave and sad. He had always been very fond of Duvall—he was fond of him still. The whole matter had hurt him very deeply.

"Monsieur Duvall," he said, without further preliminaries, "Monsieur Dufrenne tells me that you, after recovering Monsieur de Grissac's snuff box from Dr. Hartmann, deliberately returned it to him last night, in order to secure your liberty and that of your wife. Is this true?"

"Yes." Duvall's voice was calm, even, emotionless. "It is true."

Lefevre recoiled as though he had received a blow. "Can you dare to come before me, and tell me such a thing as that?"

"It was my fault, Monsieur Lefevre," cried Grace, going up to him. "Richard begged me not to tell— commanded me not to tell, but they were torturing him— they were driving him mad. Oh, I could not stand it—I could not!"

"You should have considered your duty, madame, not your husband," remarked the Prefect, coldly, then turned to Duvall.

"Young man," he said, "you have done a terrible thing—perhaps even now, you do not realize how terrible a thing. I regret that I did not inform you at the time I placed the case in your hands, but the matter is one which, at all costs, I wished to have remain a secret. Now it makes little difference. Monsieur de Grissac has for many months been carrying on with the Foreign Office a correspondence regarding the relations of France and England in the matter of Morocco. Many details of action have been settled which, in the event of certain eventualities, would constitute the joint policy of the two nations. I need hardly say that these details and policies are of such a nature as to cause, if known, an immediate declaration of war by the third nation involved. This correspondence, Monsieur de Grissac, unwilling to trust to the ordinary cipher in use for such purposes, carried on in a code of his own; one which he regarded as absolutely proof against all attempts at solution. That desperate attempts to obtain copies of the correspondence would be made he well knew, and in spite of all precautions, our enemies, by bribing a subordinate, did, some time ago, manage to secure copies of many of the most important letters and documents. Their attempts at reading them, however, were fruitless. Without the cipher, and its key, they could do nothing.

"How they ultimately learned that the key and the cipher were contained in the ivory snuff box, we do not know. Perhaps through Noel, the Ambassador's servant, although Monsieur de Grissac is positive that he never, under any circumstances, made use of the cipher in the presence of a third person. That they did learn the whereabouts of the cipher, however, we now realize only too well. When I told you that in the missing snuff box lay not only my honor, but the honor of France, I indulged in no extravagant statements. It is the solemn truth. Even now, by means of the snuff box and key which you have delivered to them, our enemies have no doubt read the stolen documents, and are preparing to strike while we are as yet unprepared." He strode up and down the room in a state of extreme excitement. "As a last desperate chance, I attempted to send you a message by means of the phonograph record. I hoped you might, in this way, learn the secret of the box, and by destroying the key, render it useless. If you hesitated to do this, fearing that, should Hartmann discover the key was missing he would refuse to liberate you, you are worse than a traitor. You are a contemptible coward. Let me tell you, Monsieur Duvall, if I had a son, I should rather have struck him dead at my feet, than have had him fail me in a crisis like this."

Grace began to weep, hysterically. "It was all my fault," she began. "I told them the box was hidden in the room below, against my husband's wishes."

"Where were you, then, that you say 'in the room below?'" asked Lefevre suddenly.

"In the laboratory, on the second floor. My husband was confined in the basement. I said I would tell—for they were killing him. He cried out to me—forbidding me to do so. Then they took me away to the room above."

"And left your husband alone, with the snuff box in his possession?" demanded the Prefect, sternly.

"Yes."

"For how long?"

"About—about ten minutes," she replied, wondering at his question.

"And you," exclaimed the Prefect, in a voice of fury, turning on Duvall, "were left alone in this room, with the snuff box in your possession, for ten minutes, at the end of which time you calmly turned it over to this fellow Hartmann. *Mon Dieu!* Why did you not destroy it—crush it under your heel—anything, to prevent our enemies from obtaining possession of it?" He looked at Duvall, his face working convulsively. "You—you are a—*sacre bleu!*— I cannot tell you what I think of you."

"Monsieur de Grissac," asked Duvall, his face white, "had I destroyed the box, or even only the key, could you have read these documents yourself?"

The Ambassador gazed at him, puzzled for a moment. "Certainly not, monsieur," he replied. "I could no more have solved the cipher than they could. It was for that reason that I was forced to carry the key about with me. But it would have been infinitely better, had the documents never again been read, than to have them read by our enemies."

Without making any reply, Duvall placed his hand in his pocket and drew out, between his thumb and forefinger, a tiny white pellet, no larger than the head of a match. "You are no doubt acquainted, Monsieur de Grissac," he said, coolly, "with your own handwriting."

"My handwriting! Naturally. What of it?" He went toward the detective, an eager look in his face. Lefevre, Dufrenne, and Grace also crowded about, their expressions showing the interest which Duvall's questions had aroused.

The detective began to unroll the little white pellet with the utmost deliberation. It presently became a tiny strip of tissue paper, not over two and a half inches long, upon which was written a series of numbers. "Is that, then, your handwriting, monsieur?" he inquired carelessly, as he placed the strip of paper in De Grissac's trembling hand.

"*Mon Dieu!* The key!" fairly shouted the Ambassador, as his eyes fell upon the bit of paper. "Monsieur Duvall, what does this mean?"

"It means, monsieur," replied the detective, coolly, "that while I was left alone in the room downstairs, I tore off the lower half of your key, which luckily, was a sufficient width to enable me to do so, and with a fountain pen I had in my pocket, wrote upon this second slip of paper a series of numbers taken at random. This series I placed in the secret recess in the box. I do not think it will prove of much use to our friends in Brussels."

"Duvall!" cried Lefevre, rushing forward with outstretched hands. "Forgive me—forgive me!" He was not quick enough, however, to forestall Grace, who with one cry of happiness had flung herself into her husband's arms. "Richard!" she cried, and then sank sobbing but happy upon his breast.

Monsieur Lefevre seized his assistant by the arm and began to shake his hand in a way which almost threatened to dislocate the young man's shoulder. "My boy," he cried, laughing and crying at the same time, "forgive me—forgive me. I was hasty. I should have let you speak, first. God be praised, everything is well. De

Grissac—think of it—they will puzzle their brains over that cipher for weeks and weeks and they will discover nothing—nothing! Is it not splendid!" He grasped the Ambassador's hand and embraced him with ardor. "Magnificent! Superb!"

The Ambassador was no less overjoyed. "Young man," he said, "we owe you the deepest apologies. No one could have done better. I thank you from the bottom of my heart." Dufrenne also offered his congratulations. "My friend," he said, "I have done you a great injustice. I salute you, not only as a brave man, but as a very shrewd one. As for me, I fear I am only an old fool."

Duvall patted the old man on the shoulder and smiled. "A patriot, monsieur, and for that I honor you. I was luckily able to turn the tables on these fellows. But one thing you, and all of you, gentlemen, should know. Had I not been able to substitute a false key for the real one, the latter would never have passed into Hartmann's hands, if I had died for it."

"I know it, my friend. I was a fool, a dolt, even for one moment to doubt it. I ask your pardon, and that of madame, your wife," cried Lefevre, seizing Duvall's hands in his. Grace looked proudly at her husband, her knowledge of her own weakness forgotten in the triumph that he had won.

"And now, monsieur," said Duvall, with a look of happiness in his face as he caught his wife's glance, "with your permission, Mrs. Duvall and myself will begin once more our interrupted honeymoon."

The Prefect put his arm about the detective's shoulder, and gave him an affectionate hug. "My poor children," he cried, smiling at Grace. "In my excitement, my happiness, I had completely forgotten that you are only just married. And such a honeymoon as you have had. It is indeed shameful, and the fault is mine—mine alone. But I shall make amends, my children. You have rendered both me, and France, a great service, and I do not forget it. I insist that to-night you shall dine with me.

You, De Grissac," he exclaimed, turning to the Ambassador, "will, I know, be one of the party. And it is not alone for the purpose of dining that I ask you, your service to France shall be acknowledged in a more substantial way. Monsieur de Grissac and myself will have the honor to present to you, Monsieur Duvall, and to your charming bride, some tokens of our gratitude and esteem. After that—go—enjoy your happiness. You have earned it." He glanced at his watch. "Madame, you are fatigued. You need rest—sleep. I insist that you permit me to send you to my house, where Madame Lefevre will have the honor to receive you, and make you comfortable. You, Duvall, can in the meantime make your arrangements for leaving Paris to-night, and also secure your baggage from the *pension* in the *Rue Lubeck* where it awaits you. I myself will accompany you, and render you any assistance in my power; we will then rejoin your wife at my house, where Monsieur de Grissac will meet us in time for dinner. What do you say?"

Grace clung to her husband's arm. "I'm afraid to leave him, even for a minute," she said.

Duvall pressed her hand, and noted her swollen eyes, her white and drawn cheeks. "You have had a terrible night, dear," he said, kissing her, "and you must have a few hours' rest. Go to Monsieur Lefevre's house, and lie down and sleep for a little while. You are so nervous you can scarcely stand. I will not be long."

She gave his arm a little squeeze, then turned to the Prefect. "I thank you, monsieur, and since my husband thinks it best, I will gladly go to your house at once. Good-by, Richard." She accompanied Monsieur Lefevre to the door.

Two hours later, Duvall, having made all arrangements for leaving Paris for London that night, descended from the Prefect's automobile at the latter's house in the *Rue de Courcelles*. Within an hour they had been joined by Monsieur de Grissac and were all seated about Monsieur Lefevre's hospitable board. Everyone was in jubilant spirits, and in the happiness of the moment all the suffering of the past week was forgotten. De Grissac presented to the bride a magnificent diamond crescent, and to Duvall a gold cigarette-case of exquisite design and workmanship, while Monsieur Lefevre, not to be outdone, placed in Grace's hand a rare lace shawl which, he assured her, had been worn by a Marquise under the Empire. To Duvall he gave a seal ring, with the arms of France engraved upon a setting of jade. "It belonged to my father," he said, simply. "With me it is a talisman; you will never ask any favor from me in vain."

When M. Lefevre came at last to say good-by to Duvall and his wife, there were tears of real sorrow in his eyes. He had no children of his own, and the happiness of his two young friends had been his happiness as well. The thought that he might never see them again left him with a great sense of loneliness.

"Good-by, my dear boy," he said, grasping Duvall's hand in both of his, as he stood beside the door of the automobile which was to take the happy pair to the railway station. "When you settle down upon that little farm in your own country, and raise the chickens, and the pigs, and, may I also venture to hope"—he smiled meaningly at Grace—"the children, do not forget your old friend Lefevre."

Duvall pressed his hand, while Grace hid her blushes in the darkness of the cab.

"I shall never forget, *monsieur*, that to you I owe the possession of the sweetest and best wife in the world. We shall meet again, I promise you."

"Good! I shall hold you to the promise, *mon ami*. And if you do not keep it"—he pointed his finger impressively at the pair in the cab—"I shall send for you to assist me in the next difficult case which puzzles me, and *voila*! The thing is done. You would not *dare* to fail me, should I call upon you for assistance."

He took Grace's hand and kissed it with old time courtliness, then slapped Duvall upon the shoulder.

"Go now, my children. If you stay longer I shall be unable to restrain my tears."

As the automobile turned the corner below, its occupants saw the old gentleman still standing on the sidewalk, gazing after them and waving his handkerchief in farewell.

"Dear old Lefevre," said Duvall, as he drew Grace to him and kissed her.

RESURRECTED PRESS CLASSIC MYSTERY CATALOGUE

E. C. Bentley
Trent's Last Case: The Woman in Black

Ernest Bramah
Max Carrados Resurrected:
The Detective Stories of Max Carrados

Agatha Christie
The Secret Adversary
The Mysterious Affair at Styles

Octavus Roy Cohen
Midnight

Freeman Wills Croft
The Ponson Case
The Pit Prop Syndicate

J. S. Fletcher
The Herapath Property
The Rayner-Slade Amalgamation
The Chestermarke Instinct
The Paradise Mystery
Dead Men's Money
The Middle of Things
Ravensdene Court
Scarhaven Keep
The Orange-Yellow Diamond
The Middle Temple Murder
The Tallyrand Maxim
The Borough Treasurer
In the Mayor's Parlour
The Safety Pin
R. Austin Freeman

Arthur Griffiths

Fergus Hume

Edgar Jepson

A. E. W. Mason

A. A. Milne
The Red House Mystery

Baroness Emma Orczy
The Old Man in the Corner

Edgar Allan Poe
The Detective Stories of Edgar Allan Poe

Arthur J. Rees
The Hampstead Mystery
The Shrieking Pit
The Hand In The Dark
The Moon Rock
The Mystery of the Downs

Mary Roberts Rinehart
Sight Unseen and The Confession

Dorothy L. Sayers
Whose Body?

Sir William Magnay
The Hunt Ball Mystery

Mabel and Paul Thorne
The Sheridan Road Mystery

Louis Tracy
The Strange Case of Mortimer Fenley
The Albert Gate Mystery
The Bartlett Mystery
The Postmaster's Daughter
The House of Peril
The Sandling Case: What Would You Have Done?
Charles Edmonds Walk
The Paternoster Ruby

John R. Watson
The Mystery of the Downs
The Hampstead Mystery

Edgar Wallace
The Daffodil Mystery
The Crimson Circle

Carolyn Wells
Vicky Van
The Man Who Fell Through the Earth
In the Onyx Lobby
Raspberry Jam
The Clue
The Room with the Tassels
The Vanishing of Betty Varian
The Mystery Girl
The White Alley
The Curved Blades
Anybody but Anne
The Bride of a Moment
Faulkner's Folly
The Diamond Pin
The Gold Bag
The Mystery of the Sycamore
The Come Back

Raoul Whitfield
Death in a Bowl

And much more!
Visit ResurrectedPress.com for our complete
catalogue

About Resurrected Press

A division of Intrepid Ink, LLC, Resurrected Press is dedicated to bringing high quality, vintage books back into publication. See our entire catalogue and find out more at www.ResurrectedPress.com.

About Intrepid Ink, LLC

Intrepid Ink, LLC provides full publishing services to authors of fiction and non-fiction books, eBooks and websites. From editing to formatting, from publishing to marketing, Intrepid Ink gets your creative works into the hands of the people who want to read them. Find out more at www.IntrepidInk.com.